S0-BAO-536

# THE HEALER

# RICK GIBSON

*Saint John Neumann Church*
*601 East Delp Road*
*Lancaster, Pa. 17601*

A JAN
DENNIS
BOOK

## THOMAS NELSON PUBLISHERS

Nashville • Atlanta • London • Vancouver

Copyright © 1994 by Rick Gibson

All rights reserved. Written permission must be secured from the publisher to use or reproduce any part of this book, except for brief quotations in critical reviews or articles.

Published in Nashville, Tennessee, by Jan Dennis Books, an imprint of Thomas Nelson, Inc., Publishers, and distributed in Canada by Word Communications, Ltd., Richmond, British Columbia.

Scripture quotations are from the NEW KING JAMES VERSION of the Bible, Copyright © 1979, 1980, 1982, Thomas Nelson, Inc., Publishers.

Library of Congress Cataloging-in-Publication Information
Gibson, Rick.
    The healer / by Rick Gibson.
        p. cm.
    "A Jan Dennis book"
    ISBN 0-7852-8132-0
    1. Spiritual healing—Fiction. I. Title.
PS3557.I22H4 1994                                    94-257
                                                     CIP

Printed in the United States of America
1 2 3 4 5 6 7 8 – 00 99 98 97 96 95 94

# Acknowledgments

I would like to thank editor extraordinaire, Andrea Stewart, who spent, countless hours editing my manuscript long before I ever submitted it to the publisher. Her top-drawer ideas and marvelous insight made the difference.

I'd also like to thank my mom, Millie Gibson, for all the years she has supported me mentally, spiritually, and especially financially. Without her, I'd have had to give up long ago. Thanks, Ma, I love you.

*"... they will lay hands on the sick, and they will recover."*

(Mark 16:18)

# 1

It came out of darkness silent as fog. There was no warning and only a fraction of a second to recognize a large mountain lion. Chills of pure terror screamed up the young giant's back and threatened to tear his hair and the Expos baseball cap from his head. There was barely time to throw up a forearm as the animal leaped for the throat's vulnerable vessels. The sound of crunching twigs played inside the boy's head as two thousand pounds of pressure bit through nine muscles and two bones.

That afternoon it had been much too hot even for the first day of summer, especially at four thousand feet. Bubbles crackled as the knobby bicycle tires rolled over boiling tar. A celebrating solstice sun was involved in a grand game of hide-and-seek with several large dollops of clouds. Whenever the clouds tired, old Sol gleefully burned shadows to cook more tar.

Both sides of the pass road were lined with stone walls shaded by maples and oaks. Robert Frost had been there, written about it some. Here and there, part of the earth's skull could be seen sticking out of crew-cut pastures strewn with switching dairy cows.

Redwings, the most plentiful of all North American birds, screeched from a prickly mountain marsh that continued to remain one field away. Elsewhere, thrushes, meadowlarks, and song sparrows polished strains that had worn well with time. Background to all was the silence of the mountains.

The only person he had encountered during the whole day of riding had been a pneumatic old woman hobbling to the road in order to check her mail. Eva Bartlett, 1023 Tinker's Ferry Road. White reflecting letters set in a rusty plate on top of the scabrous mailbox said so.

"How do you like this day?" he had called, slowing to initiate conversation.

"Too hot. Never see it this hot for June."

She answered without flavor, tending her own business. Flowers in the print of her housedress had long ago been reduced to the same lightly faded shade. Flesh from deflated biceps swung in hatchet shapes beneath arms that had once lifted sixty-pound alfalfa bales with ease.

"This country is gorgeous."

"Lilacs never knew what hit 'em." She wasn't finished with Jess's first question.

"Will this road take me to Whitecliff?" He stopped the bike but stayed on the seat.

"Been here sixty year. Never seen better. Never

will either." Still stuck one question behind, she began to warm just a little and finally looked at the young man. The rural elderly are suspicious but not paranoid like their urban counterparts.

"How far is it to Whitecliff?"

"Twenty mile, give or take."

He glanced at the falling sun, smiled, and said, "Thanks. You have a good afternoon."

He started to push off and get back on the pedals but stopped short. "Mrs. Bartlett, how did you get the bandage on your leg?" Her housedress barely covered white, pulpy knees. The bulbous wrapping on her calf was the color of old shopping bags and would have demanded anyone's attention.

"Oh, this thing. Doctor said it's some kind of ulcer, tumor . . . somethin'. They want to operate, but I don't have much account for them's with a knife. I'm eighty-two years old. I can get around. If it puts me down, so be it. Don't expect there's too much time left anyway."

He sighed silently and said, "I don't mean to be forward or frighten you, but would you mind if I take a look at it?"

"You a doctor?"

"No, but I think I've seen that kind of thing before. I may know a way to make it go away."

She began to blossom from the attention.

"You be a big one, don'tcha?" He had stepped off the bike. His grin matched her amusement.

"Come up on the porch. Bet you could use something to drink, too."

"No. Don't trouble yourself."

"No trouble. Tea's made. It's strong and cold."

"Thanks."

He wheeled the bike beside her as she slowly hobbled the thirty yards back to the house. They talked about the weather. When they reached the screened-in porch, he took his time leaning the bike against a tree as old bones claimed another victory over the gravity lurking beneath half a dozen steps. He was there in time to get the screen door for her. Its spring hinges sounded like a coffin opening in a "B" horror movie. A wave of burnt laughter floated through the inside doorway. She must have had the TV on for company.

"Thanks. Have a seat. What was your name again?"

"I'm Jess Waterson, Mrs. Bartlett. It's a pleasure to meet you."

"Pleasure's mine, assured." She pointed to a couple of green lawn chairs on the porch. "I'll just go get the tea. Don't get much company either. You ain't one of them serial rapers or something are you?"

He smiled and said, "No, ma'am. Quite the contrary."

"Didn't think so. Yer big, but I can tell."

In the half hour it took to drain the two glasses of tea, she emptied her head of saved conversation. She had no family. The nearest neighbors were a mile away, young and not very friendly. When she had business or shopping to do in town, she drove the old 1975 Buick sticking out of the rickety garage. Evidently, the only attention she received was from her cats and a few acquaintances at the church she had attended most of her life.

During the silences a persistent breeze strained itself through the porch screen. It sounded like the high end of a cheap-movie wind machine—old, eerie, restful.

"Would you mind my taking a look at your leg?"

"Guess it won't hurt. At my age, I ain't gonna worry about being too modest."

"I know you're a modest woman, Mrs. Bartlett. Modesty is read on the face, not in what you're wearing."

She blushed.

Several pungent odors swirled stronger and stronger around the porch as he slowly peeled away the yards of bandage. The last six feet came away sticky, then sopped with tang. On the inside of her calf, a putrid, open sore surrounded a purple lump the size of a tennis ball.

"Smells, don't it?"

"Mrs. Bartlett, that must be extremely painful. Why don't you get the thing treated?"

She paused, and her gaze went through the screen and across the road to spear the shimmering heat snakes in the pasture beyond the stone wall. It was a faraway voice that finally said, "Just scared, I guess. Never knew many my age that's went into a hospital and come out alive. Take my chances here. Be with my cats, my own place."

The boy leaned forward and gently touched the creped skin with his fingertips.

"I think it could use some air," he said as he straightened up. "Would you trust me and promise you'll leave the bandage off until you go to bed this evening?"

"I guess it can't hurt. It sure does tingle. Never did that before. Must be the air."

"Do you have any hydrogen peroxide?"

"There's a bit under the bathroom sink."

"Good. Ma'am, if you'll just bathe around that thing with a cotton ball soaked in peroxide and leave the bandage off, I think you'll see some improvement."

Two hours after the young man left, Eva Bartlett happened to glance at the abomination on her leg that she had lived with for over two years. She had not noticed the absence of pain. To her surprise, there was no longer a lump or a sore. In their place was healthy, pink skin. It wasn't until the next day that she noticed she was walking upright, not stooped with arthritis; that she was urinating without pain for the first time in fifteen years, and she could see clearly a world that for as long as she could remember had been perceived through cloudy cataracts. In the days that followed, there was no more irregularity in impacted and worn-out bowels, and she felt better and better as aches and pains that had plagued her for decades packed up and left.

Six miles down the road, in a stand of white pines, the young man had made his camp for the night.

Jess Waterson was a giant—six-foot-ten, two-hundred-sixty-four pounds. His nineteenth birthday was just a week away. A spectacle without his shirt, he looked as if he worked out constantly. In fact, the musculature and strength were genetic. Ringlets of golden-blond hair framed a face constructed of angles and proportions that stopped the heartbeats of women of all ages. Perhaps cheekbones that were just a little high, a ruler-straight nose, and a hint-of-cleft chin had something to do with it. Piercing, golden eyes the shade of stained and varnished oak looked at you in a way that said he was interested in everything you had ever done. Unusual for a kid.

Early summer had found the young giant riding an extremely oversized, custom-made mountain bike along the back roads and trails of northern Vermont. At the Whitecliff Post Office there would be a package of money he had mailed to himself from Europe a few weeks before. "Hold indefinitely for pickup," it said. It was money from a large grant the United States government had paid over a sixteen-month period for the special privilege of studying his unique gift. Even at the beginning, his father, foreseeing the future, had advised him to hide the money in a Swiss bank. The money was now used to stay one step ahead of the few powerful men who knew his secret.

It did not help that he looked like an angel incarnate—huge, massive, beautiful, always drawing attention when he was around people. With the batallion of private and government agents now looking for him, he was seldom allowed the luxury of lingering. Two weeks before, he had spent a couple of days in a Quebec town with a narrow, but busy, canal running through it. He'd found a room in a motel and watched the boats, enjoyed the colors, food, and people. It wasn't long before he spotted a man snooping around, asking the wrong questions. Jess had dyed his hair black and was wearing blue contacts, but they were still able to find him. He had disappeared by hitching a ride with a vacationing family who was cruising the canal in their houseboat.

With his free hand Jess grabbed the cougar by the high throat and squeezed the carotid arteries closed. The cat struggled, and the young giant held her away from him, dodging the thrashing hind legs. Instinct carefully bred through millions of years wouldn't allow her to give up the prey in her mouth, and the grip relaxed only when the brain shut down. With one arm, Jess gently lowered the unconscious, one-hundred-twenty-pound animal to the ground. A mountain lion in Vermont was as rare as a rhinoc-

eros swimming with the swans on the Swanton
Common. It must have escaped from a private col-
lection. Even in the dark Jess could see the lather
around her mouth.

*Rabies! Brain fried with fever. I knew something
was wrong. She wouldn't have attacked while I was
standing up like that. Neck's in the wrong position
on a human unless we're stooping over. Poor thing
had no idea what she was doing.* He mouthed the
words silently. The shock was quickly wearing off,
and the arm pain was gearing up. He squatted beside
the cat and gently stroked her head with his good
hand.

"Let the healing begin, old girl. You deserve better
than what you've gotten so far in life." The cat
would wake up in about an hour. When she did,
there would be no trace of rabies, no arthritis, no
more toothaches, no parasites—no more pain in her
rear legs from badly set broken bones two years
before.

"Physician, heal thyself," he said softly, as the
pain grew exponentially.

Blood dripping freely, he wrapped his mangled
arm, not too tightly, just above the elbow with the
ever-useful camo bandanna that hung around the
pedestal of the handlebar light. He then sat down
cross-legged on the dry pine needles and closed his
eyes in concentration. Carefully, layer after layer, he
folded inside himself, willing the communion of his
season. Inside his arm, foreign bacteria burst their

cell walls, bone silently melded to bone, muscle cells regenerated, and blood vessels and nerves straightened and reformed. When he finally returned consciously to his surroundings, the pain was gone. He loosened the bandanna, draped it around the light once again, then turned the light on and looked at his arm. It was smooth again. Not even a scar. Ten minutes later, he was half a night and two miles down the road. The halogen light spanked patches of tar that were finally cooling beneath an escalating breeze. Grotesque fragments of clouds drifted across an anemic three-quarter moon.

"I think it's going to rain."

# 2

"Mommy, Choctaw's hurt! He's bleeding!"

"Where is he, Jessie?"

"He's out by the road. A car hit him. I saw it! I saw the whole thing!"

The five-year-old had been playing on the front porch of the log cabin in the rolling Virginia countryside. He came bursting through the door accompanied by screams of terror. Tears flowed freely as he pulled his mother from the kitchen, down the hall, and out the front door.

Stephanie Waterson picked up the little boy, who was large for his age, and ran to the edge of the lawn where the family's large yellow and white cat lay in a limp pile.

"They didn't even stop, Mom." The words came jouncing out.

The nurse put her son down and reached for the cat.

"Choctaw? Say, old fellow."

The cat looked at her with eyes half closed by its inner eyelids.

"We'll have to take him to the doctor, Jess. Run and get me a towel from the bathroom. Quickly!"

"Is he gonna be all right, Mom?"

The sobs had stopped, but tears still streaked down the angelic face.

"I don't know, honey. Go—quick! We'll have to let the doctor see." She could see at least two limbs bent at odd angles, and the cat was bleeding from his ears and mouth. There were a couple of deep cuts.

In less than a minute the little boy was back with a towel. His mother carefully wrapped the broken animal and handed him to Jess.

"You get in the back seat and hold him. I'll go call the vet and tell them to set up for an emergency."

She quickly returned and found Jess on the back seat holding the blood-soaked bundle on his lap. The car peeled rubber for ten feet beyond the driveway.

"You know, Jessie, Choctaw doesn't look too good. He might not make it. Do you think you can deal with that?"

"He's gonna be all right, Mom. He'll make it."

*Oh, boy!*

"But, honey, you don't want to get your hopes up too high. He's very badly injured."

"It's okay, Mom. He'll be all right."

"Jessie, listen to me. Things don't always turn out the way we want them to. Sometimes we lose loved ones. You remember Grandpa Davidson." On the verge of recklessness, she negotiated several country roads in order to turn onto the main road into Annandale.

"I know what you're trying to say, Mom. I'm five years old." The child was precocious for his age, but he had never faced a death before. Sometimes Stephanie became frustrated with his pragmatism. Sometimes it got him into trouble.

"Jessie, I really don't think he's going to make it, and you'd better prepare yourself for that!"

He didn't answer. When she glanced in the rear-view mirror, she could see that his eyes were welded tightly together. *He'll just have to learn*, she thought.

She short-screeched to a halt in the parking lot, jumped out, and opened the back door. Jess handed his mother the limp bundle, and she bolted for the door. The boy remained in the car with the door open.

"Hi, Stephanie. What's old Choctaw done this time?" The doctor and two veterinarian nurses were waiting for her with the door open. She handed the bundle to the vet and said, "A car hit him. He doesn't look too good, Andy."

"We'll see what we can do." They disappeared through a pair of swinging doors, and Stephanie looked around for Jess. She found him still sitting quietly in the back seat of the car, eyes still squeezed tightly together.

"The doctor's got him, honey. We'll just have to wait." She climbed in beside her son and sat quietly. Everything she could say had been already said. Anything else would fall on granite ears. After half a minute, without opening his eyes, he took her hand and said softly, "He's gonna be all right, Mom. Don't worry."

Twenty minutes later, one of the nurses beckoned to Stephanie from the front door.

*Uh-oh. Too soon.*

She leaned over and kissed the little boy and then reluctantly made her way up the steps to the office. The vet was waiting for her, holding the cat in his arms.

"Steph, what did you say was wrong with him?"

"Jessie said he saw the car hit him. I know the old fellow had two broken legs—probably head injuries. There were cuts, too. But you . . ."

"What else?"

"Andy! He was bleeding . . ."

"I know," he interrupted. "From the ears and mouth. We washed some off his fur too." The vet massaged the old cat's forehead with his finger. Stephanie could hear Choctaw purring from four feet away.

"Steph, there isn't a mark on him. No broken legs, no nothing."

"WHAT!" She reached to turn Choctaw in the doctor's arms so she could see the large cut that had been bleeding so badly. In its place was healthy orange and white fur. No wound—not even a hint.

"Here. I think you nurses work too hard." He handed the cat to her.

"What in the world!" She turned the cat around a couple of times, examining him closely. Choctaw gave her a weak mew of protest.

"We x-rayed him head to foot. Everything's intact. There isn't a crack to be found. He doesn't even have a bruise. You sure about all this?"

"But . . . You saw the blood on the towel . . . on his head."

"I don't know where it came from. Maybe the bottom of the car from some other animal. It wiped right off."

"Andy, I know he had two broken legs!"

"You want to see the X rays?"

"The cuts that were bleeding . . ."

The doctor simply looked at her and said nothing. She said the perfunctory good-byes and carried the cat back to the car. Jess was standing beside the open door. He stretched out his arms and cried, "Choctaw!"

The mother handed the cat to the little boy, who hugged it to himself carefully. Choctaw nuzzled and wedged his large orange head between the child's upper arm and side. The cat hated riding in the car, and with his head buried he didn't have to watch the countryside flying by.

With a mind full of questions, Stephanie closed the door behind her son, got in, and pointed the car toward home.

The trip to the post office at Whitecliff began routinely enough. Jess picked up the padded mailer he had sent to himself under another name and in care of general delivery, then headed to the bike. He slipped the envelope under the bungy cords that held the pack to the rear luggage carrier, mounted the bike, and headed for the park across the street. Picking out a secluded bench, he opened the mailer and found his four thousand dollars in twenties and fifties. He took a risk sending cash through the mail, but any other way left a trail. He stuffed most of the money into a waterproof zippered compartment in the pack and headed for the local supermarket.

Inside the post office, Roger Gordon, one of the postal workers, stood looking out the front window with a cordless phone in one hand and a colored photocopy picture of Jess in the other. Above the picture it read, "Not for publication." Below, "Have you seen this man? Reward—$50,000—call the NSA." It gave a U.S. government number that would ring in a large office building about fifteen miles northeast of Washington, D.C. The postal worker punched the buttons, and the switchboard operator answered on the first ring.

"National Security Agency."

Jess stuffed the groceries into the bike saddlebags and rode on the sidewalk down the main street for a block. He stopped beneath a giant oak that had been living long before Ethan Allen conscripted his Green Mountain Boys. Leaning the bike against the tree, the young giant dug his satphone out of the bike backpack and dialed another number that rang in the same suite of offices but bypassed the switchboard.

The familiar gravelly tenor voice answered, "Bartholomew."

"Forget it, Nathan. You'll never get anyone here in time."

"Jess! When are you going to quit fooling around and get back here where you belong?"

"Yeah, I know—my country needs me. Nathan, when are you and your boss going to give up trying to deprive me of my natural-born, all-American, constitutionally guaranteed freedom, et cetera, et cetera?"

"Jessie, all is forgiven—trust me! The president is prepared to give you your freedom, and we'll pay you well if you'll just help us out once in a while."

"Your idea of freedom and my idea of freedom, if I remember rightly, are a trifle incompatible." *And the day you could put two sentences together without lying . . ."*

*An uncomfortable feeling began to tug . . .*

"I know. Looking back, I'll have to admit we've both handled this thing all wrong. I'll fix that. You can come and go as you please; just let me know how to get in touch so we can use your services when there's a crisis."

"Like when the president gets another cold? Or a congressman gets a bad case of a social disease that doesn't respond. Come on, Nathan. *Homo sapiens* and his ancestors got along just fine for several hundred thousand years without me. I'm enjoying myself out here."

"But there are times when you could be of great help, Jess. You can't negotiate world-class disarmament treaties if you've got the flu and feel like green dog puke."

*. . . at the back of his mind . . .*

"Yeah, I know. Or if you've got tennis elbow and it's interfering with the cocktail circuit. Nathan, I want you to quit pressuring Dad. Threatening to hold up his retirement checks isn't really going to break him, but I don't like where you're going."

"Jeff Waterson can take care of himself. I needed you to help save a man's life. Your dad would not tell me where I could reach you, and you wouldn't answer your satphone. Incidentally, the man died. He was extremely important to our intelligence coming out of Hungary. It's a shame we lost him. He had a wife and three kids."

"Sorry. I don't want to appear calloused, but like I said, the Lord giveth, and the Lord taketh away, and sometimes he has the gall to do it without consulting me. Give everybody my best, Nathan. Listen, I need to hit the road. I don't want to make it too easy for you, do I? I imagine that your little flyers with my picture on them are in most of the post offices in the United States by now. And you're not shelling out fifty grand just for the privilege of buying me lunch at McDonald's. . . ."

*. . . and it was getting stronger . . .*

"Jessie, if you won't answer our calls, at least call me once a week or so, will you?"

"Maybe." *When they hold Olympic skiing in Kansas.* "Good-bye, Nathan."

The satphone didn't come cheap, but it was untraceable. While the phone ringer was turned off, a caller ID program stored the numbers of the last fifty people who had called. If the number of his parents or someone he wanted to talk to appeared on the tiny, scrolling screen, Jess called them back. The others, like Nathan, were discarded.

He put the phone back in its water-tight bag and replaced the bag in the pack. Then he got on the bike and continued riding slowly down the sidewalk, admiring the hundred-year-old homes with their verandas, arbors, and gazebos and the venerable old sugar maple, oak, and elm trees that protected all. The feeling of forgetting something tugged at him briefly, and then the familiar routine of fastening a car safety belt came to him.

"Hope they never figure out how to make it mandatory for bikes."

The freedom of the mountain bike was a never-ending pleasure. The smells, sounds, and vistas to be experienced went by much too fast and noisily in a car. The twenty-one-gear bike could fit through places a motorcycle could not, and it never ran out of gas. It could be carried effortlessly across streams and wheeled up steep hills where there was no trail. It could be hoisted up and down cliffs or lifted over obstacles that would stop a four-wheeler. It could be dissasembled and thrown in the trunk or back- seat of a car or on a plane or bus. As long as there were no chase scenes, Jess had an edge, and there was no way he was going to allow anyone close enough to glimpse him, much less chase him.

*Wrong!*

### . . . *and stronger!*

The young giant turned up the narrow village street labeled "Bridge Street." The street had led him to the main street, and he knew it was the shortest route back into the mountains. About half a mile from the middle of town, an iron bridge spanned a narrow gorge. Jess had stopped on the bridge on his way into town.

*Black water. Deep. Got to be some good trout down there, but how would I fish it? Too swift for a boat. Sides are sheer granite—nowhere to even stand.*

Not one, but two Vermont State Police cars came screaming into town from opposite ends! One of them came within fifty feet of Jess as it raced down the main street for the post office.

*Judas! Why did I have to show off on the stupid phone! Too much time!*

A large yard between two white-clapboarded houses afforded a quick glimpse of the middle of town. Jess could see Roger Gordon standing in the middle of the street gesturing wildly. The man was pointing at Bridge Street.

The boy was still a quarter mile from the bridge when he heard the roar of the cruisers. They had turned onto the street and were accelerating fast. At the far end of the bridge, the road began its ascent on the mountain, and the hills were far too steep to climb at more than a crawl. There were no side streets, and Jess knew he was now in plain sight.

On the ramp to the bridge, there was a four-foot lip outside the guardrail. The young giant hit it doing almost thirty. The earth dropped from beneath him, and he remembered thinking, *I'll bet it's going to be very, very cold!*

It was. In spite of the summer heat.

Jess hit the water in a sitting position, and the bike landed about five feet from him. Custom made, the mountain bike's frame and rims were made from superlight honeycombed polycarb. Gears, pedals, and chain were machined from titanium alloys, and the whole bike, without packs, weighed less than fifteen pounds. Regardless of how light it was on land, it would still sink like a rock.

"Got to have the bike!" Without transportation, money, clothes, and survival tools, he'd be a sitting duck in the mountains.

Mentally gasping in shock from the icy water, Jess allowed himself to sink feet first as he tried to intercept the bike on its path to the bottom. The river was deep, and he sank fifteen feet before he felt himself being skipped along a rocky bottom by the current. The pressure popped his ears, and he could see nothing in black water that was blocked from the sun by the walls of the gorge. The young giant fought the relentless drift and groped frantically in every direction for what seemed like hours.

Nothing.

Jess badly needed air, but if he surfaced, the bike would fall behind him and he'd never find it. The panic of suffocation began to set in, and just as he was about to spring off the bottom in a desperate sprint for the surface he felt his hand brush cloth.

*Pack!*

He lunged with his other hand and felt the seat post slip away as the bike caught on a rock and stopped bouncing along the bottom. His lungs began to involuntarily expel the poisonous carbon dioxide in tiny spews as the boy planted his feet, braced against the current, and once more grabbed wildly. This time he brushed the crossbar, and lunging desperately, he grabbed it tightly with both hands. He pushed hard off the rock bottom, expecting to be on his way to the surface, but he almost lost his grip when the bike refused to budge.

*Current must be wedging it against something on the bottom. You've got to have this bike, Waterson! You're as good as caught without it!*

Air expelling more violently now, Jess pulled hard against the current and managed to get his feet planted on the upriver side of the large boulder that had trapped the bicycle. Once more he yanked and the effort squashed the last pint of air from his lungs. Brain starved of oxygen, the young giant felt an instant giddy high as the bike finally sprang loose. Water now streamed down his nose and throat, and after a thousand years he broke the surface, prize in tow.

Exhausted, half coughing, half vomiting, he had one last glimpse of the bridge before the current took him around a bend. The cruisers' strobes flashed angrily behind the old bridge's intricate ironwork. Two troopers stood at the railing, and one of them was speaking into the radio handset. Jess wondered if there'd be a reception committee waiting when he got to wherever it was this little expedition was taking him. The walls of the gorge were high and as perpendicular as the side of a building. There was no way to get out of the water until the shoreline flattened out.

Strength gone, the boy knew he couldn't keep the bike afloat for very long by treading water. Holding the frame with one hand, he unzipped a pouch on the side of the saddlebags and took out a plastic trash bag. The bags were handy for a number of uses beside trash. Laid across boughs, they made a good roof against the rain, and he could sleep on them if the ground was damp. He opened the bag and whipped it above his head to fill it with as much air as possible; then he knotted it shut like a balloon. Following the same procedure, he inflated four more bags. Using the bandanna, he tied them to the bike's crossbar. The bags were nowhere near full of air, but there was enough buoyancy to keep the bike from sinking.

By the time he was able to get out of the water, Jess almost wished there'd been a reception committee. The current had taken him through a half mile of canyon, then several hundred yards of sloped banks too steep to climb before the gorge finally relented. On one side, the shoreline reluctantly flattened into a pasture. The other side had not given up so easily. The wooded slope of a large mountain rose with quiet regality from the water.

The pasture was cut in half by a gravel road that led to a small dock, and Jess was elated to see a battered aluminum runabout swaying gently in the river's mellowed current. An equally beaten-up ten-horse Johnson guarded the boat's transom. The boy pulled the bike out of the water and let it fall. Freezing and exhausted, he flopped onto his back on the dock and gazed into a stone-washed June sky.

"High cirrus—good weather for a couple of days. At least something's in my favor."

Within five minutes, his breathing was normal and his strength had returned. The mark of good conditioning in an athlete is not how tired he—or she—gets, but how quickly breathing, pulse, and strength return to normal. Jess was in excellent shape.

"Come on, Waterson. They'll be here any minute."

From the bike's pack, the young giant took out a small sandwich-sized Zip-Loc bag. He placed six fifty-dollar bills in it along with a note that said, "Rent for one runabout with motor—three hundred dollars. Thanks." That was considerably more than the boat and motor were worth. He left the bag in plain sight on the dock after placing a small stone on top of it to keep it from blowing away. Then he lifted the bike into the boat and pushed off. The motor started on the third pull, and instead of heading downriver, the boy headed straight to the opposite shore. The bank was steep but not impossible. From his pack he removed a fifty-foot length of rope and tied it to the bike. Tying the other end to his belt, Jess scaled the slope about twenty-five feet and found good footing. Then he lifted the bike out of the boat and pulled it up the bank to him. The boat quickly drifted away from the shore and headed downstream in the current where it disappeared around a bend. Hopefully, it would float a long way before it was found—all the more territory they would have to search. They would never expect him to be on the mountain across the river from where the boat had been docked.

Jess was only a hundred feet up the slope when one of the police cruisers skidded to a stop at the dock. The young giant was not about to take any chances and was ready for them. Even hidden as well as he was in the mountain foliage, he quickly covered the bike and himself with a sheet of camouflage cloth. One flash of sunlight off the bike's chrome . . . If they sent helicopters he would use the same routine, although the trees were more than thick enough to protect him. He would also be invisible if they used the helicopters to search the woods at night with infrared nightscopes. The cloth had been treated with the same chemical the army uses to treat combat fatigues. The chemical prevents the soldier's body heat from showing on the scope.

From a hundred and fifty yards across the river, Jess watched the trooper pick up the note on the dock, get back in the car, and turn it around in the pasture. The wheels spat gravel for two hundred feet before the car disappeared over a hill in a cloud of dust.

Wheeling the bike through the trees and around the bare rock, Jess climbed through the afternoon. There would be no more carelessness. If they caught him, they would lock him up for a long time, and Uncle Sam would make certain that there would be no more escapes.

"Interesting fungus there. Well, Mr. Waterson, sir, let's take a short look."

The logging road swam in late-afternoon shadow as Jess leaned the bike against a large bass tree. He took one of the two water bottles out of its holder and took a long drink. The water had come from a small crystal-clear stream about a mile back. Soon he was engrossed in the fawn-colored fungus on a fallen log. Cicadas—tree toads they called them in Vermont—buzzed like miniature chain saws over-head in the hardwoods. The mysteries of Mother Earth were never-ending, and even in the heat of retreat, the young man's curiosity was insatiable.

# 3

Nathan Bartholomew had an ear to the ground in the rapacious center of American government. Very little went on that didn't come to his attention by means of a variety of sources, all of whom were keen on ascending the ladder of power. Having survived the brutal climb for eleven years by spiking the backs of the weak and gutless, he had leveled off as the head of the National Security Agency, personally hand-picked by the president. The brilliant young planner was only thirty-five, and it didn't take him long to broaden the powers of the glorified code manufacturing and deciphering agency into an organization that dabbled in all aspects of national security. It was not without credentials that he had climbed through the ranks. At twenty-three, he had already earned a Harvard doctorate in behavioral psychology, studying in a department that was the brainchild of B. F. Skinner himself. Postdoctoral work had included working on a top-secret government project that streamlined the manipulation of the masses in national emergencies by using the media—even if it meant resorting to the use of subliminal television messages. Shame, shame! When the U.S. went to war, it was absolutely vital that the public support the president and Congress as near to 100 percent as possible. The Vietnam disaster had never been forgiven. Grenada had seen the rough influences of using a controlled media; Panama had seen a little more improvement. The war with Iraq had shown signs that they were starting to get the hang of it, and by the time the "invited" marines had invaded Colombia, then the southeast provinces of Burma, then the series of small Caribbean states—all havens for drug lords and their products—the American public was dancing to the music, and Nathan Bartholomew was playing first fiddle in the band.

The young Jewish behaviorist had fallen in love with the way the U.S. government could not only create but also cut red tape. He was infatuated with the power Uncle Sam was capable of doling out. He went back to school and in two years earned his doctorate in political science and a master's in international relations. With an IQ in excess of 185, this was not a difficult task for the little bulldog from Brooklyn who stood five-feet-five and weighed 125 pounds soaking wet. Added to the intellect were charm, cunning, and an astute common sense that made his ideas and proposals fit like a glove.

Nathan had learned of Jess Waterson's secret purely by accident. Agent Bartholomew had been working for the FBI Department of Behavioral Science at Quantico at the time. He'd been drafted temporarily out of his department to pull an all-nighter listening to "possible disaffected" surveillance tapes. Because one of the staff was on vacation, two had the flu, and another was in the hospital with appendicitis, someone had to keep the backlog of listening material from becoming an insurmountable mountain.

The yacht of a prominent Washington attorney had been bugged, and Nathan was skimming through the tapes looking for evidence that might point to the attorney's collaboration with the stubborn Chinese who were dragging their feet on an embargo against North Korea. The man had the ear of the president, and there were rumors the attorney's boat was going out much too often with Chinese-looking types on it.

Unknown to Nathan, the attorney had loaned the fifty-two-foot boat to the Waterson family for the weekend. After listening for only a few minutes, Nathan discovered that the lawyer was not on board. The agent was about to fast-forward the tape when something in the conversation caught his attention.

"Jess, if you're going to use your gift to heal somebody in as bad shape as Frankie Ryan, you're going to have to figure out a way to do it so there'll be absolutely no way for you to be connected to his recovery—as if anyone would believe what you do is possible anyway."

"I know, Dad. If they find out, we'll never have any peace. I can see the consequences, especially for you and Mom. Our house would be a cross between an Oral Roberts service and the cathedral at Lourdes. But Frankie is so neat! He deserves a chance at life. There's gotta be a way."

"Steph, come here a minute."

"Yeah?"

"Jess wants to help Frankie Ryan."

"You mean that quadriplegic boy?"

"Yeah. Jess says they've just diagnosed the kid with brain cancer. In addition to not being able to move, he's gradually going blind. The chemotherapy alone . . ."

"Oh, mercy. That poor kid."

"We need to put our heads together and figure out a way Jess can do it without drawing any attention. This will not be like curing acne or football injuries or some of the other things he's been pulling for years. This might turn into national news, and it's bound to raise questions. Any ideas?"

Bartholomew heard the woman's voice again. She said, "Nobody deserves a load of misery like that— especially not a kid. Just losing his folks in the accident would have lasted most people a lifetime." She paused a few seconds, then continued, "I don't know, how about if Jess healed him gradually—over a period of weeks; I'll find out who's treating Frankie and strongly recommend the experimental lab at Johns Hopkins. There's a new program using tactile electronics to bypass damaged nerves. And we know that it's not unprecedented that cancer goes into permanent remission. The experimental stuff would be a good setting for a medical miracle—cover a multitude of sins." There was a hint of a smile in her voice.

"Sins—yeah. Jess and sins."

Jess had always been so deeply involved in church activities and helping other people, he hardly had time for sin. He was the epitome of "good" so his parents were mildly amused by the thought.

"What do you think, Son?"

The boy seemed to ignore the teasing. "Who's to say it would be impossible. Mom, will you talk to the doctors on Monday?" There was no mistaking the excitement in his voice.

Nathan went back and replayed the tape. Then he erased it. The next day he easily found out whose family had been on the attorney's yacht. He also kept tabs on Frankie Ryan, who over the next four months miraculously began to walk while he recovered totally from terminal brain cancer.

Under the same "possible disaffected" cover, Nathan had the Waterson home bugged for a month, allowing no one else to come anywhere near the tapes. Nathan Bartholomew, mover, shaker, learned all he needed to know to provide himself with a huge accounts-receivable voucher somewhere down the road, maybe from the president himself. He made sure he was introduced to the Waterson family, and from then on he kept an eye on the family's twelve-year-old miracle worker.

Four years later, firmly entrenched and looking for more maintenance points with his boss, Nathan approached Jeff with a deal to set up a program to study Jess's incredible ability. "Jeff, this miraculous gift should be shared. Let us study the boy. Let's see if there's any way of replicating the ability—chemical, physiological, gene splicing—whatever. Who knows, we might discover how to totally wipe out disease, pain—it's mind boggling! Millions of lives may be saved!"

Nathan refused to tell where the information about Jess had come from, but Jeff knew that sooner or later his son's secret had to get out. It never occurred to him that the craft he had dealt in his whole military career had been the means of discovery—that the Waterson family actually had done a good job of protecting their boy's miraculous abilities.

The men haggled.

"You know if you don't agree, we'll take him anyway under the National Emergency Act. This information is too vital to this country to selfishly remain only in the hands of your cozy little family. If we take him by force, I'll make him inaccessible to you and his mother."

"That's what they call kidnapping, Bartholomew. It's illegal—or hadn't you heard?"

"Not around here it isn't."

"There's always the news media."

"Won't work. When it comes from the right sources, they back off. Something about the executives personally not liking detailed FBI investigatons and IRS audits."

Jeff had known he was beaten before they'd even started. He offered the inevitable compromise. It was what Nathan had been waiting for. The head of the NSA played the part by tipping back in his chair and putting his hands behind his head. "Let's hear it."

"You could never force him to perform on command, but you could make things miserable for everybody. Jess has agreed to give you his services for one year. It will not be cheap. In fact it will be bloody expensive. In turn, you will not only meet our financial figure, you will also provide him with the accelerated learning he needs—college tutoring, computer access, et cetera."

"Not a problem. We would have done that anyway. What's your price tag?"

"For one year—one year, Bartholomew, and this is his idea, not mine—I'd fight you. You get him for one year; he'll let you study, prod, poke; he'll perform on demand. In return, you pay into a numbered bank account in the city on the pretty lake in the Alps the bargain figure of $3 million—tax free."

"We'll do it."

"You're kidding!"

"No, we want to find out what makes him tick. Actually, the president has authorized more than that."

"The president!" Jeff paused, then said, "Well, I suppose when it means the nation's number-one hypochondriac gets a free cure every time he gets a sore throat, he would—especially when it's the taxpayer's money."

The day after his sixteenth birthday, Jess entered the special wing of the Walter Reed Army Medical Center on part-time status. He would graduate from high school in six weeks. He was mostly looking forward to the learning the government could provide him. There would be unlimited sources to be tapped by computer and by private tutors. He could get lessons in courses from calculus to cooking. At last he could get the learning his mind craved at the high-powered rate he was capable of absorbing it. He fully intended to take the government just as much as it would be taking him.

To Stephanie and Jeff Waterson, the birth of the precocious child who was now about to graduate two years early from high school had been an unplanned surprise. Jess could have graduated much earlier, but both father and mother had insisted that the boy's social development was important enough to keep him in grades where the kids were near his own age. Jess was born when his brother Jimmy was fifteen and his older brother John was a sophomore in college. Stephanie and Jeff had been well entrenched in middle age, although Stephanie had steadfastly refused to show it. She was forty-four when she started missing periods; Jeff, forty-eight. Then came the morning sickness.

*No, can't be,* Stephanie thought.

It was.

Sixteen years after her third son's birth, the nurse was still turning heads with her natural-blonde hair and flawless skin. Her figure was as perfect as it had been in college. She looked thirty-five and showed no signs of aging or slowing down. She was a constant source of amazement to those around her, including her husband, who had a hard time keeping up with her. She was also one of the most beautiful women Jeff had ever seen. Hazel eyes smiled, with or without the trace of crow's feet, from a face that belonged to the girl next door who grew up to be a beauty queen but who never needed all the makeup and pampering most beauty queens do.

Jeff had been a twenty-five-year officer with the Navy. A graduate of Columbia University's seven-year law program, he had spent most of his career in Naval Intelligence. After retiring, he continued with the Navy another twelve years as a consultant while he started a private law practice. At sixty-two, he quit consulting to concentrate on his practice. He maintained his contacts with the government and, from time to time, was still called in as a consultant.

Jimmy worked for a computer company in Washington. He was married and had two kids. Older brother John was thirty-five and divorced. He was a high school math teacher and soccer coach.

Stephanie had worked in the huge Walter Reed medical complex for over twenty years, but it was Jeff who had brought his son to the research wing of the hospital that first Saturday morning. Jeff wanted to see what Uncle Sam had up his sleeve.

Stephanie already knew some of the staff who would be testing her son. A special basement suite of labs would accommodate the long-term program required to dissect and document the teenager's incredible gift. The doctor who met them at the security door labeled "Top Secret—No Entry" was sixtyish, six-three, sandy-haired, and freckled. His face was barely large enough to support the infectious ear-to-ear grin.

"Jess! And how do you do, Commander. I'm Donny Lee Fielder. I'm the chief honcho for this little wingding." A large paw was quickly offered to both father and son. "I'm Navy, retired, like you, Commander." The drawl was definitely Texan, and the man didn't sound unlike Jimmy Dean. "Come in and meet the other campers. I've worked with your little wife on several occasions. She's one of a kind."

Father and son were introduced to a nurse, a physiologist, a statistical psychologist, two technicians, and a secretary.

"C'mon in and set a spell."

Jess and his father were led into an office without windows. The walls were painted government green.

"Jessie, Nathan's been telling me about you for quite some time now. I know you've been reluctant—I sure would be—but we've got an incredible opportunity to learn some things that really might make a difference. It's sort of like a shipload of space aliens landing and offering us a few secrets to the universe."

Jeff let his son do the talking. Jess looked the doctor in the eye and began. "Doctor Fielder, it's not out of selfishness that we've tried to keep this in the family. You must realize what the cost would be to me and my family if the secret about my abilities got out. The first thing that would happen would be my mom or dad, or one of my brothers or friends— maybe somebody I don't even know, would be kidnapped by the mob, or, heaven forbid, a government—ours or theirs. The ransom would be for me to cure somebody's terminal cancer or maybe just a bad case of the flu."

"I know this, Son. We've taken all kinds of precautions to keep it between the fences. I certainly don't want the responsibility of robbing you of a normal life. The results may be used or published or whatever, but I give you my word of honor I'll never tell a soul who you are, and if any of my staff let the burro out of the barn, the next chance they get to flap their gums will be in permanent solitary confinement at Leavenworth—with no TV!"

"I'm glad you understand. How will you go about the testing?"

"Most of what we want to do can be done in-house in conjunction with the projects we're working on anyway. There are a few experts we'd like to bring in. They've done other things for us that needed to be kept secret. For instance, one of the neurologists who will look at the results is the famous Sean O'Reiley. You see him on the evening news every once in a while. He'll fly in from Boston General. The blood man comes from Cleveland. The pathologist is on our staff here—Terry Balswen. So is one of the endocrinologists—Bob Seacabart. There are several others who live right here in town—DNA boys, shrinks, IQ, chemistry, microbiology, electricity, particle testers—all experts in fields we want to explore. All are operating under the Official Secrets Act. They will sing with very high voices and never father children again if they tell anyone about this project. All are excited, unbelieving, skeptical. We want to take you apart, young man, and find out what makes you tick."

The doctor finally stood up and said, "What I'd like to see today—and you're gonna have to forgive this ugly ol' Texan who was born too close to the Missouri border—I'd like to see you do your magic, right before my li'l ol' eyes, without the aid of smoke and mirrors."

Jeff stood smiling. Jess merely stood and said, "Fair enough. Where? What have you got?"

"Do you mind if the other staff members watch this?"

"Not at all. That's what I'm here for."

The doctor pressed a button on the phone and said, "Wendy, get everybody and meet me at the corral quick as skat will you?"

A confirmation came back over the phone. He stood and said, "Follow me." Jess and his father stood and followed him across the room.

The doctor opened the door and started down a hall painted in more government green. As he walked he said, "We've got a whole hospital full of sick people within the radius of a few hundred yards here. However, we don't need anything that dramatic. Besides, when we put you to work on humans, we want it to be under controlled conditions." He opened a door, turned on a light, and continued speaking. "About an hour ago, on my drive into work, I saw the car in front of me hit a possum and keep on going. Now I don't know about you, but it hurts the fire out of me to see animals suffer. I stopped and looked the little feller over. He's got a broken leg and some cuts and bruises. Don't let the veterinarian association know, but I gave him a pinch of phenobarbitol and brought him in to work with me. I'd planned on having someone take him over to the vet wing at U of M—I have a couple of friends over there. However, this is a much better idea. Why don't you just go ahead and fix him up for us?"

Jess wondered how much of what the man was saying was true but decided there was no reason, at this point, to doubt his word. They entered a large room that contained a number of empty cages. The doctor threaded his way down an aisle to a large wire cage sitting on a table. Inside was the opossum, barely awake, one of its hind legs bent at an errant angle. There were a couple of bare patches of bloodied skin.

"Well, Jess, what do you think?"

"Doctor Fielder, will all the animals we work on be injured or sick from natural causes?"

"You have my word on that, son. I don't cotton to experiments on animals. I know, I know—it's necessary, and over the years animal research has saved millions of lives. But let somebody else do it. For our little tea party, we don't need to hurt anybody or make anybody else sick. There are already thousands of patients in veterinarian clincs and hospitals that need desperate help. My wife gets mad at me sometimes for taking the mice away from our cat and carrying the little tykes back to the field. If I can let it out the door, I won't even kill a fly."

Jeff, who had been quiet up to now, said, "Doc, I think you and Jess are going to get along just fine."

Jess walked to the cage and opened the door. The other members of the staff had entered the room. They crowded around to watch. The boy reached in and gently stroked the animal's coarse fur. The opossum looked at him with large, dark eyes that were devoid of fear. Jess scratched behind its ears, and the pink, bare tail swished once in what could have been pleasure.

The people watching saw nothing out of the ordinary. Just a boy petting an opossum. They couldn't see the three broken segments of bone fuse and the break disappear as the large, soothing hand carefully slid down the leg and adjusted the skewed angle; nor the reddened and bruised skin return to normal as fingers passed over the scrapes; nor new, coarse fur quickly spring to life over smooth skin where there were once open cuts. The animal's metabolism had been speeded up ten thousand times, but dopamines and natural tranquilizers had been increased accordingly to keep it from blowing itself into tiny bits.

Jess reached in with his other hand, took the opossum in both hands and said, "Come on, lazy, get up."

The animal stood and nudged the boy's hand. From his pocket Jess pulled out a packet of peanut butter and cheese crackers. He unwrapped the cellophane and placed them on the floor of the pen. He brushed the animal on the head a few times, withdrew his hands and closed the door.

"You mean, that's all there is to it?"

The opossum attacked the crackers as if it hadn't eaten in a week. Soon it was walking energetically around inside the cage, sniffing, looking for more. Both hind legs were perfectly normal.

"Holy Moley, Sapphire! That's all you have to do?"

Jess turned to him and said, "I can control how long it takes to restore the tissue. I can make it happen over a period of time, or I can speed it up and make it happen in just a few seconds."

The other staff members were crowding around the cage, leaning over and exclaiming to each other in voices as controlled as possible.

Jess continued, "I think the ability to stretch the process out came as a defense mechanism. It allows me to escape detection. If I'm not around by the time the patient is completely healed, they can't pin it on me, and I can maintain my anonymity."

"I was expecting bells and whistles and shoutin' and fireworks! You just will it, sobeit, in your mind?" The doctor was duly impressed.

"That's about it. Sorry about the fireworks."

"That little feller hasn't even got a scratch on him. Look at that! I ought to be disappointed, Son. You were supposed to scream, 'Hee-yell!'"

# 4

They finished the tour of the suite and its labs in half an hour.

"Bartholomew was supposed to be here but got stuck in the middle of some kind of crisis. He'll take our word. I've planned on a couple of weeks to give you a complete physical and mental workup. You can come in after school. Obviously, you should graduate with your class even though we could arrange for you not to have to. We need to quantitate your mind and body in as much detail as possible before we start testing you during your little thaumaturgic demonstrations."

Jess grinned at the doctor's referring to his miracles as magic.

Fielder continued. "We need some benchmarks to compare. No sense of whipping the nag before we get in the carriage. When we do start testing for real—and I'll tell you again, I'm impressed—we'll probably start with the very simple—worms, insects. We'll run blood and wave tests, scans—all those goodies—on both you and the patient while you're at work. We'll work up to the more complex—birds, mammals, primates—see if there's any difference in your body when things get more complicated. We'll be monitoring the patients too, of course. We'll see if there are cycles to your effectiveness, maybe even see if you're capable of reversing the process—making well animals ill—only enough to tell and temporarily, of course. Like I said before, I don't like that end of the business."

Up until then, that idea had never occurred to Jess.

"I don't have to remind you that you've already signed the Secrets Act. I think that was a little superfluous after finding out how long y'all have kept this thing under your hat. After what I've seen, I don't disagree. If I were you I certainly wouldn't want every Tom, Dick, and Bobby Lee comin' up to me and demandin' my services at the point of a gun—or worse. It wouldn't take very long to kick the hound in the creek." There were times when Donny Lee Fielder's drawl thickened effectively.

On the following Monday after school, Dr. Fielder and his staff began their in-depth testing. Every school afternoon for the next two weeks and for six hours on Saturdays, the scientists collected what Fielder called "their pound of flesh." Blood, urine, saliva, *succus entericus*, stools, bile, semen—any fluid or tissue that could possibly be sampled was. Biopsies were taken, capacities were measured.

There were electrocardiograms, electroencephalograms, X rays, CAT scans, ultrasounds, neutron scans, digital laser sampling. The boy was poked, peered into, and pried open—right down to the molecular level.

"Jessie, your body has some very exciting . . . what'll I call them? Mutations, I guess. We've found some astounding things."

"For instance?"

"Your cell structure is much denser than normal—say, on the order of ten times as dense as mine. Where my cells would be mostly water, yours are smaller and more compact—less fluid." Doctor Fielder was keeping Jess informed as Jess had requested. "Yet you don't weigh any more than a boy of your size should weigh, and cell nutrients and waste actually circulate better than in a normal human. Compared to yours, our bodies are incredibly inefficient. Some of the structures in your cells are a real hoot. We have no idea what they do. Your DNA is a total enigma. It'll take centuries to unravel. The real question is, 'Where did you get it?' I've quizzed your mama; she says there's a chance that she might have been inadvertently exposed to X rays or something experimental when she was pregnant, but she's just as puzzled as we are."

The young giant took it all quietly, shutting off his mind and allowing them to perform the necessary abashments and humiliations. These same people would be doing this against his will if he'd not "volunteered." He concentrated on composing and sequencing the list of subjects he wanted to study, especially those that would require tutors. There were so many fields to explore—everything from ancient religions to modern nuclear biochemistry, military strategies, astronomy. He also thought of the freedom the money would give him and the learning he'd be able to access no other way.

"We've found that your brain is as much a puzzlement as the rest of your body. It, too, is much more dense, but the electrical patterns—how shall I put this—instead of flowing randomly, they flow in complicated micro-pulsed patterns. Totally amazing! The doctor who did your first electroencephalogram thought his machine had gone berserk. He hasn't been able to measure properly because his machinery isn't calibrated in the right strata."

After the physical tests came the mental evaluations. Several psychologists sampled his mind and his ratiocinative processes. It was not difficult for Jess to hide those abilities that he did not want anyone to know about.

At the end of two weeks they announced that the macrotesting was temporarily finished. They had enough to run with. As soon as the young giant was through with school, they could begin the study full-time. He already had access to a private room with a computer terminal. With the list of subjects he had given them, they scheduled computer time and the tutors he had requested. It was decided that he would roughly maintain a thirty-hour-a-week work regime. The remainder of the time was his own only if they didn't need him. Theoretically he was on the government payroll and on call twenty-four hours a day, seven days a week. When not working, he was allowed to go home.

Eight A.M. on the Monday after graduation, when Jess arrived at what he had jokingly begun to call his office, there was an expectancy in the air.

"Well, Jessie, are you ready to quit foolin' around and go to work?"

Jess gave Fielder a grin and said, "What a nice vacation. I'd recommend this place to anyone who just wanted to get away."

Fielder had maintained a good rapport with Jess, as had most of the staff. They had made it as painless as possible, and Jess knew that. He was aware that his gift was unique and that natural human curiosity needed to be surfeited as well as possible. Had he been in their shoes, he would have wanted to know the same thing—what makes this human able to heal in the space of a few minutes, or hours, what is entirely outside the realm of modern-day medicine? How can tissue be regenerated simply by willing it? What an incredibly miraculous gift this young man has! Where did he get it?

"Then let's get to work on some 'them li'l ol' sick critters we been collectin' and see what you can do with them."

Jess grinned at him and said, "Cain't daince. Maaght jist's well."

The first three months they hooked him up to all kinds of monitors and had him perform his magic sometimes for two or three hours a day. While they were readying the next experiment, the young giant studied on the computers. Once or twice a week, Stephanie dropped by to see what they were doing to her son. Jess wasn't spending much time at home. After hours the tutors came in, sometimes until the wee hours of the morning. Then if there was time, he went home to sleep and reported again in the morning at six. If not, he caught a nap on a cot in one of the storage rooms. Getting along on three or four hours of sleep did not particularly bother the teenager, who was still growing physically at an alarming rate. At age sixteen he was six-foot-five. He could always catch up on his sleep on the weekends. There were also the "seasons," he called them—periods when no one was allowed to interfere—periods spent meditating, renewing—precious time spent in communion with his source.

The research staff began the tests by using diseased insects and worms. From there, they moved on to small water animals sickened by exposure to toxins in their environments. Some had been injured physically by predators. Jess often wondered what the collectors were told. He watched carefully to make sure none of the animals had been crippled on purpose, and he was never given cause to suspect. Dr. Fielder apparently had applied strict regulations to the specimens, even the simple ones.

Next came the fish and then birds. During each healing his body was subjected to a battery of scans and rays. They found that the enigmatic brainwaves and electrical patterns did indeed change from animal to animal, and the patterns depended on what kind of wound or disease the animal had. Broken bones and wounds were usually repaired like the opossum's—by speeding up the animal's metabolism. However, at will, Jess could do it by other means. Infectious diseases might be treated by a select electrical bombardment of the invading organism, which ruptured cell walls and nucleii. But there were a number of other ways to do that, too. His hands were capable of generating infrared heat, low-level X rays, myriad electrical codes and impulses, and several other sources of wave and radiant energy. The young giant seemed to have a storehouse of techniques to get the job done, and many of them were a complete puzzlement to the scientists.

"Can you do plants?"

"Yes."

A whole new series of tests were run on plants. Beginning with diseased algae, they ran the entire gamut of flora all the way to diseased hundred-year-old trees. Jess restored the plants to health as effortlessly as he healed the animals.

After five months they were ready to begin on the

mammals. Jess freed mice, squirrels, numerous dogs and cats, whole herds of cattle, an elephant, two Siberian tigers, various kinds of monkeys, one ape, a duck-billed platypus, and a vast number of other animals from the bonds of disease and trauma. Zoos and veterinarians in a six-state radius were called upon to donate their unresponsive diseased and injured. The animals were returned in perfect health, and no explanation was given in spite of numerous questions.

"Ma, I'm having a ball. Don't worry about me. And I'm getting plenty of exercise. I'm working with a tae kwon do instructor from the FBI four times a week, and I'm playing tennis with a couple of the doctors on staff."

"But don't you miss your friends?" Stephanie was basting four Cornish game hens that would be part of dinner. It was late Friday afternoon, and Jess was home for the weekend. He continued to investigate his first quality meal of the week. Most of the time he ate in the hospital cafeteria or local junk-food restaurants. He lifted the cover from a kettle of soup slow-simmering on the kitchen stove and smelled.

"Tom Sharfe, Dicky Ramos, and I are going to the shore next Saturday. They'll catch me up on what's going on with the guys. Ma, I've got almost unlimited access to learn anything I want to. I holler 'nuclear pretzel bending,' and the next day there's a nuclear pretzel bending expert knocking at my door.

I could never get all this stuff in college. They hook me up to the monitors, I do a little healing, then I'm free for the rest of the day to study or whatever. Last week they took me through the 'hand-to-hand' at Quantico. Then the firing range—I fired seven different kinds of weapons."

"It all sounds too good to be true. I just worry. Nathan Bartholomew is going to drop the other shoe sooner or later, and that grimy little creep doesn't do anything that isn't in his own selfish interest."

"Well, I'm going to make the most of it while it lasts. I've got Thursday and Friday off next week. There's a conference most of the staff are attending in San Diego. I thought maybe I could talk Dad into going to the mountains to do some trout fishing. Wanna come?"

By the end of eleven months they were ready to begin on *Homo sapiens*. The mammal testing had not gone as fast as expected. There were some equipment failures, but mostly, the enthusiastic scientists kept coming up with new experiments, new attempts to quantify and qualify the elusive power. Also the lab testing had to be done in-house by the staff. A commercial lab would raise too many questions. Many of the chemical analyses were time-consuming and required a number of cook, cool, add, separate, cook, allow to stand, add, boil, skim, centrifuge, etc., cycles. Already there were file cabinets full of stored computer readouts and hundreds of computer rams. Jess Waterson became the most documented person in the history of the planet and would remain so for a long time. But they still didn't know how he did it. His personal studies had ranged over dozens of topics, each digested with ease and totality, and he was always hungry for more. So when they offered him another $3 million for another year, he took them up on it. No school could provide him with the concentration he was capable of handling along with the incredible variety of subjects. He wanted to know about everything from how the Salk vaccine worked on polio to how they manufactured dulcimers in a rural town in Kentucky. He studied reciprocal-engine mechanics along with quantum mechanics. He studied the martial arts, the art of war, the thespian arts, and the culinary arts. He studied how they manufactured paper, plastic, pepper, polycyanides, pralines, and a multitude of other materials. He studied the organic chemistry in organic farming. Most of the learning was digested faster than it could be taught. He stayed up all night working with equal interest on a computer program or a study of the life cycle of a tapeworm found in Japanese fish. Nothing escaped his interest, nor was he denied access to anything except classified information.

Three months into his second year Jess met the sheikh. It was when the foundation began its first soft crackling, its small pieces crumbling beyond repair.

# 5

It was the end of September, and the shadows of the tall medical buildings stretched farther and thinner across parking lots and quadrangles. Petulant at the reduced daylight, millions of quarts of chlorophyll had gone on a six-month strike leaving the leaves to strut their true colors.

The scientists had started Jess healing humans in the middle of August. The young giant had grown perceptively taller in the last fourteen months. He was now six-foot-eight. He was considerably stronger than anyone of his size should have been, and his quickness was on a par with a handful of karate film stars whose movements are so fast the final edit is slowed to let the audience see more than just a blur. It was all in that complicated DNA code.

Dr. Fielder and his staff began Jess's tests on human patients with simple skin problems—warts, rashes, poison ivy, psoriasis. The doctor made calls to ask a few local dermatologists for referrals. The doctors were told that the FDA was testing some new wonder drugs. Jess then saw the patients in one of the hospital's examining rooms that had been connected to the monitors in the lab. The monitor leads required to document the healing physiology of the young giant had been miniaturized. Well disguised beneath his clothes and hair, they relayed their information by way of microtransmitters. There were no telltale wires. Jess could walk around freely. Fortunately, his size seemed to overcome any skepticism about his age, so he was always introduced as a medical student. He had grown skilled at pretending he was only assisting the doctor in the examination. He smeared the patient's skin with a placebo salve, the ingredients supposedly still a secret. The results, as always, were miraculous as the patient's diseased skin was transformed into a perfectly healthy and normal condition.

It was one of the last mornings in October when Jess turned at the sound of accelerating footsteps to find Nathan Bartholomew trotting across the parking lot. Nathan had observed the experiments from time to time, but had never turned up at six in the morning.

"Jessie!"

"Morning, Nathan."

"You ever see such a change in temperature?" A Canadian cold front had dropped the temperature into the teens. The NSA agent's breath scalded the early morning air in great clouds.

"Colder than tin Jockeys, Nathan."

They made small talk through the corridors to the

elevator, then down the long basement hall to the special suite. Nathan led him to Dr. Fielder's office. The agent hung his overcoat on a rack in the corner and began rubbing his hands to warm them.

"So tell me, how are the tests going? They treating you all right around here?"

"We seem to be almost on schedule, Nathan. I think we're about to graduate from the skin diseases. I'm not sure what Doc has up his sleeve next."

"How are your folks?"

"They're fine, Nathan. You probably know better than I do. You didn't come here at this hour to discuss me. What's on your mind?"

Nathan sighed and said, "The state department's got a problem I think you may be able to help with."

"You're paying the salary, Nathan. I'm just the hired hand."

"You're more than that, Jessie. We've grown extremely fond of you. I was hoping we'd never come to this situation, but here it is."

"Sounds grim."

The head of the NSA walked around behind Dr. Fielder's desk where he'd set his attaché. He took out a manila folder and opened it to reveal an eight-by-ten-inch color glossy of a middle-aged Arab dressed in a suit and fez. The man's dark beard was salted liberally with white. He was looking at the camera but turned enough away to reveal a tremendous hooked beak. The nose was punctuated on either side by the piercing mahagony-colored eyes of a ferret.

"This is Sheikh Ali Herami Noorda Harb. He's the son of a wealthy Moroccan prince, spent the first part of his life in the Sahara Desert. He graduated from Harvard summa cum laude and has never looked back. Worldwide, he owns a number of highly successful enterprises, several of which supply Israel with necessities they can't get anywhere else—products like oil derivatives that are the basis of a dozen life-saving medicines. He owns several metallurgical factories in Europe that supply the Israelis with exotic metals they use in a number of industries. Over the years, the way he's handled himself has brought a great deal of respect from the Jews. Right now he's on the cutting edge of getting them to sit down with several Arab countries to talk about not trying to remove each other from the earth with the enthusiasm they've displayed since Father Abraham. So far, no one else has had any success, including several good men from this country who've tried. He's the only person we know of that both sides trust, and there may not be anyone else for a while. He's a remarkable man. I know him well, went to school with him."

He handed the picture to Jess, and the young giant studied it for a moment.

"Jessie, I imagine you've guessed what's coming. We just found out last week that he's dying from an inoperable malignancy in the middle of his brain. Have you ever tried anything on that order?"

"Once."

"Some state department officials are leaving tomorrow morning to go see him. There is some unfinished business. I'm going with them because he's a personal friend. I'd like you to come along and see what you can do. The president has given us an okay. He's the only one outside of the people in the lab here who knows about you."

Jess thought to himself, *Yeah, I wonder what the president knows about me, Nathan—and exactly how the both of you are going to work it to your advantage.* In spite of the man's charm, Jess had never trusted the NSA agent and never would. It was no secret that a handful of the patients Jess had healed under the pretense of research were high-level diplomats. This was the first time Nathan had just come right out with it.

"Do you think you could help my friend?"

"I won't know until I see him, touch him—shake hands."

"If worse came to worst, Jess, I believe the sheikh is a man who would keep your secret."

"No, thanks, Nathan. There'll be another way."

"So be it. What do you think the chances are?"

"I'm not sure, Nathan. Because the tumor's in the brain, once the healing process begins, his behavior may not be predictable." *At least it won't be if I think you're conning me.*

"How so?"

"Once the tumor is gone, depending on exactly where it is, the surrounding cells are going to be released from the pressure they're under now. He could act perfectly normal; he could go to sleep; he could scream and rave like a maniac for days, weeks. It would probably only be temporary, but there's no guarantee. The surrounding cells might return to normal after a few days, but who knows?"

"Would he be in pain?"

"No. The brain feels no pain. But it doesn't react like other parts of the body. It's the difference between fixing a broken remote terminal of a large mainframe or fixing the mother board. The brain tolerates fooling around with the rest of the body, but it gets a little perturbed when it's involved itself."

"It's absolutely amazing to me—this gift. With all this research, we still don't know how you do it. Do you visualize the tumor? Visualize its shrinking?"

"Sometimes." Jess handed the picture back to him.

"There'll be three other men going with us. Tom Oliver's an undersecretarty of state. He'll have a couple of aides—attorneys probably. A state department jet is scheduled to take us to Switzerland tomorrow morning. The sheikh is at his mountain home right now. To begin with, it's at twelve thousand feet, and there's snow all year around. He has an oxygen mixture piped into the ventilation along with the heat. You won't believe the place even when you see it. "

Jess didn't. The house was the size of a large warehouse—there must have been a hundred thousand square feet. It sprawled on numerous levels across the top of a snow-covered mountain. The only access seemed to be by helicopter. Jess was reminded of a couple of James Bond movies. If for some reason they had to effect an escape, he hoped it wasn't by skis and parachute.

"Nathan, what's that?" Jess pointed to a long, gnarled silvery ribbon leading from one end of the complex down the mountain and out of sight.

"That's Ali's bobsled run. He talked me into going down it with him once. Never again."

"It must be three miles long."

"It's closer to four and a half. The top is natural; toward the bottom where the temperature gets warmer in the summer, it's maintained artificially. It ends at his garage on the edge of town. He keeps all his cars and snow vehicles there. Obviously, he can't keep them up here. The run isn't used much any more. Over the years several people have been killed on it. Ali now prefers to go down the mountain in a helicopter. So do I."

"Might be fun." Well, at least there was a better escape route than skiing off a mile-high mountain using a British flag for a parachute.

The helicopter circled the sprawling roofs once as

the pilot picked up the wind direction from three different windsocks. Interpolating all three, he finally set the chopper down on the pad with only a slight jar.

"Nathan!" The Arab was waiting in his shirtsleeves on the helipad as the men disembarked. He stretched his arms out to embrace Nathan. Jess and the three diplomats waited patiently.

"Ali, old scoundrel, friend."

The sheikh was a much larger man than his picture showed. Jess could see that his color was not good, and in spite of all his bravado in greeting his guests, he seemed a little shaky. Nathan introduced Jess as a friend, and with the Arab's handshake everything became clear to the young giant. Horrible images of torture and killing flooded the boy's brain. Whatever this man had purported, he had no intentions of getting the Arabs and Jews together. The closest thing to peace in his mind was when he counted his money from selling arms to both sides. Ever suspicious, Jess had suspected that Nathan might lie to him. Certainly the head of the NSA knew the truth. The young giant was the son of an intelligence agent, and his father had taught him that in the circles of government you believed nothing you were told until "the check's in the bank and it don't bounce." There was another reason they wanted the murderer alive, and Jess was not a little curious as to what it was.

Nathan didn't know that the boy's gifts went

beyond the act of healing, and Jess wasn't about to let him find out. The young giant would have to handle it without the NSA agents finding out that he knew what this monster did for a sideline—exploit and kill innocent people by starting and fanning wars in order to sell arms; spy—for and against the United States; sell desperately needed food and medicines to poor countries at enormous profits; glibly assassinate those who stood in his way. The list went on. It was all there in the man's mind. Nothing was hidden from the young giant's quick search.

"Gentlemen, as you can see, Allah has been good to me. Welcome to my humble abode. You can freshen up, and then we shall have a simple supper."

Evidently, Allah had been very good. Jess was shown to his suite, and it was like something out of a movie. There were five rooms including a small kitchenette and a sun porch with a hot tub overlooking a spectacular view of the Alps. The sitting room was huge—the size of a small house. The high, vaulted ceiling was supported by massive, rustic, stenciled beams. The bedroom ceiling was low, intimate, and upholstered in tucked and pleated silk. An enormous bed sat on a stage surrounded by a filmy silk screen. Connecting through a hall was an oversized bathroom. The room's walls and floor were covered in green marble. The tub appeared to be cut from one large block of lapis lazuli. All the bathroom fixtures were gold-plated.

Everywhere, Persian paintings and elaborate needlepoint works hung from dark, wood-paneled walls. There were several glass cabinets and numerous scrolled stands, tables, and pedestals holding intricate carvings and exquisite statuary that carried the Mesopotamian motif from room to room. If the rooms of the other men were anything like this . . . How could a man accumulate that much money and spend it all on himself?

"Mr. Waterson, supper will be served presently. Is there anything I can do to make your stay more comfortable?" The servant had knocked and Jess had opened the door still in shock.

"Maybe a road map and global positioning satellite assistance."

"Pardon me?"

"Just kidding. This place is bigger than Disneyland."

"It is one of the master's larger homes."

"Exactly how many homes does the master have?"

"It varies. Thirty or forty, I suppose."

Jess followed him to the dining room where the table looked long enough to land a small plane on. The "simple supper" was an experience the young man would never forget. After a scallop soup, they were served a garden salad arranged on a flat plate in an artistic study of greens and yellows. The vegetables were coated with a light garlic sauce and accented with real saffron. The main course was stuffed pheasant—each guest presented with his own in a flaming brandy sauce. The birds had been stuffed and partially roasted, then grilled on a hickory flame under a basting of honey and olive oil. Each entree was circled by a ring of new potatoes and link sausages boiled in sweet Italian red wine. The potatoes had been drilled and threaded by alternating sausage and asparagus stalks to form a chain around each bird. Toasted cinnamon-bread wedges topped with creamed goat's cheese, molded in the shapes of animals, were served on a plate arranged in interesting patterns with sesame sticks and dill sprigs. There were side dishes of a dozen other vegetables and fruits served with spiced sauces and dips that defied naming.

After dinner the sheikh and his guests retired to the great room. It was the size of a small gymnasium. Two servants took orders for cocktails, and Jess was, for some reason, not surprised to see his host drinking with the others. Most Arabs, being Muslims, did not drink alcohol. However, Jess knew this man was a hypocrite in more ways than one.

During a lull in the conversations, the sheikh glanced toward the young man sitting on a sofa reading a magazine and loudly exclaimed, "Allah, forgive me for my inconsideration!

"Jess, I had almost forgotten my manners. Please allow me to personally show you some of the simple pleasures available under this humble roof." He held his hand out to the young man and said, "Forgive a sick, old man and come, follow me."

Jess smiled back at the man and got up to follow.

When dealing with a snake, act like a snake. They went through one of the many doors that studded the great room and proceeded down a series of corridors.

"Nathan tells me you're helping him in some medical research projects."

Jess answered, "Yes. He talked me into it."

"I can imagine exactly how Nathan talked you into it. He and I go way back. We've driven many camels to market. He told me that your father at one time was in naval intelligence?"

"Yes. He's retired from the government. He has a law practice now."

"How interesting. And your mother?"

"She's a nurse."

"Tell me about your future plans. You're very young . . . you must still be in high school. What about college? Medical school? How about professional basketball?"

Jess grinned at the reference to his height and replied, "I graduated from high school over a year ago. I'm on an accelerated tutoring program under the auspices of Washington University. I could earn an academic M.D. by next fall."

"Allah preserve! Seven, eight years of schooling— a doctor inside of one year?"

"Not really. The practical courses, like the labs— chemistry, physics, anatomy, that sort of thing— they have to be worked out on a non-accelerated basis. Then, of course, there's an internship. We're working on those kinds of things now. The degree really isn't horribly important to me. Learning about the human body is."

"You must indeed be a brilliant young man. No wonder Nathan has taken you under his wing. What kind of medical research, if you don't mind my asking?"

"Forgive me, sir, but it's classified."

"How clumsy of me not to have foreseen."

They arrived at a long row of French doors. The sheikh opened one of them to reveal an olympic-sized swimming pool. The walls were covered with spectacular murals of mountain scenes done in tiny mosaic tiles.

"There are swimming suits and towels through that door over there." He pointed. "Please allow me to show you some of our other entertainments."

There was a bowling alley, a combination archery and pistol range, a room lined with arcade games, a medium-sized gymnasium with Nautilus equipment outlined by a small running track, a fencing room, a small theater with all the latest movies and VCR tapes, and a music listening room. Jess had yet to see a woman in the house. However, Arab homes were kept quite segregated when strange men were around.

"I must return to the other guests. We have some business to finish. Please relax and enjoy yourself."

Jess thanked him, and the Arab left him in the billiard room. It was amazing how the most lethal men were usually the most charming. The sheikh was a good example.

An hour later Nathan found the young giant in the library reading *A Short History of Afro-Arabian Law*. The book was three inches thick. Nathan surreptitiously pointed to his lips to signify that the room was probably bugged—with both cameras and microphones. He made small talk with Jess, mostly about the house, then caught Jess's gaze, lowered his head, and raised his eyebrows as if looking over a pair of glasses. It was an unspoken question: Can you heal him?

To Nathan's consternation, Jess answered verbally. "Maybe. A handshake is all I need. I won't take responsibility for any consequences."

Nathan tried to hide his puzzlement and did not answer immediately. The boy's reply was not what he wanted to hear out loud or conveyed in secret. Finally, he said softly, "Do it."

Neither spoke on the way back to the great room, where the conversation was in the midst of the usual topics—world economy, work, families, vacation spots.

Tom Oliver, the undersecretary of state, was also a man of considerable charm. He was talking skiing with the sheikh and a couple of the shiekh's aides. Oliver was in his late forties. Dark brown hair, thick and wavy, was cut to predictable government length. A slightly humpbacked nose separated friendly green eyes punctuated with crow's feet. He was well tanned and appeared to be in excellent shape.

Derry Sterf, a Washington attorney, was in his late thirties. He looked Scandanavian—light hair, light blue eyes. He was twenty pounds overweight, pounds his five-foot-six-inch frame struggled with. He had a sandpaper voice that made people want to clear their throats when they listened to him. Jess and Nathan entered the room just as the attorney was helping himself to another plateful of after-dinner hors d'oeuvres.

Jess marveled at the man's ability to eat after the incredible feast they'd finished just a couple of hours before.

The other aide was an international law attorney with a practice in New York City. His name was David Beckerman, and the few times he said anything at all, the words came out wet and slippery in a boxy Bronx accent. Jess had heard him and Nathan discussing Adagios, a restaurant on Flatbush Avenue in Brooklyn, where the cheese Danish was two inches thick and the diameter of a small dinner plate.

At ten o'clock, the sheikh rose from his large overstuffed chair and said, "Friends, it is a matter of great regret, but my physical condition requires I call it a night. Please excuse this unforgivable discourtesy. It has been a great pleasure spending the evening with each of you. Breakfast will be served at eight o'clock. The servants will see to all your needs. Good night. Sleep well."

The Arab shook hands with Nathan and the other

three men, saving Jess until last. "Jess, Nathan must be proud to call you friend. You are welcome in my home any time Allah permits you to come." He took Jess's hand in both of his and Jess smiled and thanked him. Inside his head the young giant mouthed, *Let the healing begin, good buddy. This may be the last time anyone is welcome in your home for a long time.* The Arab wasn't the only one who could smile and stab at the same time.

The sheikh turned and started for the door to his quarters. After only a few feet, he faltered sharply and caught himself on a marble pedestal that held a large, iridescent teal-colored vase. The vase tipped, fell, and shattered. The sheikh clung to the pedestal with both hands, his head down. He finally said softly, "So sorry for this despicable display. Please excuse my weakness. I did not think it had progressed quite this far." Two servants materialized immediately along with two men Jess had not seen before. Both new men were Arab, large, and dressed in dark suits. As the coat of one of them flopped open in the process of trying to get the sheikh upright, Jess saw the Uzi machine gun in a shoulder harness. There were more apologies, and finally the Americans were politely escorted to their rooms.

It was a little after five the next morning when the door to Jess's room burst open and three Arabs wearing suits barged in. One of them was holding an Uzi at an unfriendly angle.

# 6

The man with the gun screamed, "What did you do to him? *What have you done?*"

Jess had been waiting for them. He was sitting quietly in one of the overstuffed chairs. Knowing it would be a while, he had slept for a few hours. He got up, showered, and waited quietly for the fireworks to begin.

The bodyguards approached angrily, and the man with the gun again screamed, "What did you do to him? Was it poison?"

Jess looked at the man as if he were carrying a plate of barbecue rather than an automatic weapon. He said calmly, "What's wrong with him?"

"You know what's wrong with him. Was there some kind of poison on your hand? He has been getting steadily worse since he touched you. An hour ago he went into violent convulsions. Our beloved prince—foaming at the mouth like a rabid dog, screaming, tearing at his head." The man's voice was so intense it cracked and splattered as did his spittle.

Jess wiped the spit off his face with his sleeve. He kept his voice low, in contrast, as he said, "He also touched four other men. Why are you accusing me? Maybe his own stuffed-pheasant chef poisoned him."

"We examined the surveillance tapes, and we saw you and heard you talking with the Jew in the library. The security in this house is complete." Evidently it wasn't as complete as they thought it was or they would have grabbed the Americans as they left the library.

Jess stared the man in the eyes and said calmly, "Why don't you get him to a hospital if you don't know what's wrong with him? Why accuse me?"

The man slapped the young giant across the face with a blazing backhand and screamed, "You young whelp, because of you he is in the hospital right now. In this very house is one of the best equipped hospitals in the world along with three of the finest doctors money can buy. There is no cause for these symptoms. You will tell me what kind of poison you used, or you will beg me to kill you within the hour."

Jess did not allow the blow to register, which made the Arab all the madder. It was as if the man had done nothing.

Again the young giant replied dispassionately, "Where's Nathan? Maybe he has some answers for you."

"Nathan and his friends are under guard. They

will be executed one by one if we don't find out what you've done!"

Jess knew that wasn't quite true. With the slap, he had taken from the man's mind the fact that one of the aides of the undersecretary had already had his neck broken in the attempt to force Nathan and the diplomats to tell them what had been done to the master. Because the doctors could find no cause for the convulsions, the bodyguards were sure it was something the Americans had done. They took the initiative on their own, and they had no intention of letting any of the men go, even if it meant the house would be nuked by the American military. The Arabs would have their revenge. Plans were hastily made to let all five men die in a tragic helicopter crash on the way down the mountain. Jess also took from the man's mind the location in the house where the prisoners were being held.

He looked at the furious Arab and said, "Fine. Kill them. They mean nothing to me."

"You son of a dog, stand up!"

"You won't like it if I do."

"STAND UP!" The Arab's scream was so intense, dribble oozed down his bottom lip and across his chin. He threw another haymaker at the boy's face, but it never landed.

The other three men would never have believed an eighteen-year-old, six-foot-seven-inch boy could move that fast. Jess's right hand was less than a blur as he knocked the Uzi out of the man's hand. The young giant's left hand grabbed the Arab's hay-maker and stopped it in midair. Before the surprised man could even blink, Jess was on his feet. In one continuous motion the boy put the full leverage of his size behind a right-hand blow to the man's stomach. The Arab folded like a letter and flew backward into a man standing behind him who was in the process of drawing his gun. Unlike the movies, where the villains always wait in line to attack the hero, the third man charged at the boy while grab-bing for his holstered weapon. Jess covered the six remaining feet between them before the man's gun could clear his coat. The Arab was lifted high over the boy's head and effortlessly whipped fifteen feet across the room where he blasted through a large picture window overlooking the mountains. The leader started his first retch from the tremendous blow to the stomach as the man he'd landed on was untangling himself and trying to draw his weapon. With his instep, Jess kicked the man in the head, and the force of the blow carried the Arab four feet before the side of his face hit the floor with a loud splat. That left only the violently vomiting leader, who had managed to get to his hands and knees.

"You want to tell me where they are?" Jess al-ready knew where they were.

Between retches the man managed to say, "Son of a whore's dog, I spit on your grave."

"You might just as well. You spit on my face."

The young giant cupped his hand, stiffened it, and

brought the karate edge down sharply on the side and base of the man's neck, making sure not to collapse the jugular vein and carotid artery or the esophagus. In spite of what the movies and TV show over and over, it's stupid to hit a man in the face with a bare fist. The highly intricate bones of the hand are nowhere near as strong as the head bones. The Arab was driven to the floor totally unconscious. He would have a stiff neck for a week. Although it would have been just as easy, Jess had not killed any of the men. The man who'd gone through the window was lying unconscious in a snowbank just a few feet below on the ground. Jess went out through the sun porch door and brought the unconscious Arab in so he wouldn't freeze. The man had several minor cuts but nothing that wouldn't stop bleeding on its own. The boy laid him on the sofa. Then by touching all three men and willing it, he placed them in comas that would last a couple of days. It would be foolhardy to allow them to recover and enter into the chase the young giant knew was inevitable.

A number of Arabs in suits were hurrying up and down the halls of the enormous home, many of them carrying weapons openly. Each time Jess sensed someone coming, he was able to duck inside the nearest door. The one time there was no door handy wasn't a problem. Jess took the Arab by surprise as he turned a corner and left him in a darkened storage room behind several boxes of carpet shampoo and laundry detergent.

Outside the room where the Americans were being held, there were two Arabs with Uzis on slings. It was amusing to Jess that as much as the Arabs hated the Jews, most of them were using Israeli guns.

Fortune smiled—one man was lighting the other's cigarette.

"Got a camel whip on you?"

Jess had managed to get fifteen feet from the guards. They looked up in surprise . . .

"Whoops!"

. . . just as the boy apparently tripped hard on the thick hall carpet.

"Whaaa!"

He flailed wildly at the air, trying to catch his balance, spinning legs, running forward on the brink of a head-over-teakettle. Greatly amused at the giant's clumsiness, the men relaxed just long enough to allow Jess within range of his tremendous reach. The young giant straightened, grabbed both their heads, and in the timeworn head basher, knocked their heads together. There was a loud "thwack" that sounded like two large blocks of wood being knocked together, and before the men could slide to the floor, the young man caught them around the middle and carried them to the makeshift prison door.

"Nathan!"

"Jess?"

"Stand back, and I mean stand back."

"Affirm!"

Jess gave the door a pile-driving kick, and it blew off its hinges. He carried the two unconscious Arabs into the room and dumped them on the floor.

"Wanna go for a bobsled ride, Nathan?"

"Jess, it's still dark out. You gotta be kidding."

"It's either that or stick around for breakfast. You got a better idea?"

"Who's going to steer?"

"You are, Nathan. Chicken?"

"All that and much more. They killed Beckerman. Broke his neck—slowly. Inch by inch."

"Why didn't you tell them, Nathan?"

"I did, but they wouldn't believe me!"

Jess smiled.

Nathan continued as he guiltily spewed out, "They thought I was joking, making it up. Don't trust a Jew and all that." The little man's mind boiled in a cauldron of thick emotions. He mourned the loss of a colleague, and he was furious that the employees of an old friend were actually trying to kill them. If the sheikh knew what was going on . . . However, that did nothing to lessen the chances that they might all be dead in a few minutes. He also wanted to know what Jess had done to the Arab as badly as he'd ever wanted to know anything his whole life. It would have to wait. He couldn't ask in front of the other men.

The smile gone, Jess said, "I'm sorry Beckerman's

dead, Nathan. It hurts me. However, we'd better look to the living. I'll steer. I have good night vision, and Dad took me down the bobsled run in Lake Placid a couple times. There must be a four- or five-man sled in the shed." He started out the door and down the hall in the general direction of the bobsled run. "Come on! This might be fun." The men were hesitant.

The decision was made for them when three Arabs came running around a corner, machine guns leveled. Jess heard the burst of fire a microsecond before he felt the concussion and heat at his side. The Arabs grunted and flopped spastically to the floor like stuffed dolls, smoking holes trailing across their chests. He turned in surprise to see Tom Oliver, the undersecretary, with an Uzi he'd taken from the guards.

"I spent twelve years as a Marine. You want to see more?"

"Come on," Nathan yelled. "They've got to know we're loose now. Maybe they won't figure out where we're going!"

Nathan guided them the rest of the way to the bobsled shed. They could hear shouts in the hallways, and some of the noise wasn't very far behind.

"This is it, I think."

The metal door was locked, and Nathan fumbled with the deadbolt and drawbar.

"Better hurry it up, little guy, or they're gonna catch us here in the open."

They burst into the large shed, and Jess quickly found the light switch.

"Derry, get that door open!"

There were three sleds on the wooden floor. The aide ran to the large sliding door, unlocked it, and began sliding it open to the subfreezing night air. Jess was wearing a bulky ski sweater, but none of the other men even had their suit coats on. Jess, the undersecretary-ex-Marine, and Nathan lifted the longest sled onto the snowy ground and guided it to the sprinting track that led down a slope for about fifty yards. A couple of powerful spotlights set on high poles illuminated the area revealing its starting gate set off to one side. In the not-too-distant shadows, the men could see where the ice-block walls of the run marked the point of no return.

"Dump the other sleds!"

"No time! Get on!"

Jess jumped on the sled in the forward position and grabbed the padded steering cables. His long legs were seriously cramped inside the sled's streamlined nosepiece. The other three men began pushing the sled frantically just as several Arabs burst into the shed. The undersecretary hollered, "I'll do the brakes! Jump on Nathan . . . Derry!"

With no metal cleats on their shoes, the pushing was not as effective as it should have been. The little agent fell as he was scrambling onto the sled and Tom Oliver picked him up quickly by the belt and dumped him onto the seat. The ex-Marine was the last to jump on, and he made it just as the automatic weapon fire opened up. Even over the rattle of the sled's runners the men could hear the sizzle of the bullets flying over their heads. Ice chips spat viciously as scores of nine-millimeter rounds chipped and ricocheted off the ice. The sled rumbled in the open for an eternity before it entered the run proper, and just as they hit the first bend to the right Oliver gave a loud "Hut!"

"Hit?"

"Yut."

"Bad?"

"Shoulder! Smarts!"

"Can you brake?"

"What are you going to do if I can't, change places?"

"No! Learn how to fly—real quick!"

The walls moved by faster and faster as the sled went through thirty, forty, fifty miles an hour. The sun was only thinking about awakening, as the hint of an alpenglow began to break over the mountains in the distance.

The first banked curve appeared, and Jess took a shaky line through it. He was beginning to get the feel of the sled. The men felt themselves pushed into the seat from the centrifugal force, and as they came off the curve, the run dropped at a steeper angle, and the speed began to pick up seriously.

"Whoaaaaaa!"

Fifty-five, sixty . . .

Another curve loomed ahead, and Jess steered the sled too high around the eight-foot banked wall. The sled balked and jerked its way back into the solid ice trench, careening off one of the three-foot walls.

"We're all gonna die!" The little NSA man was not enjoying himself.

The sled continued to pick up speed on a long straightaway, and as they reached the next turn they heard several pops in the distance behind them. Nathan turned around and shouted, "The morons are coming after us! I didn't think anybody else could be this crazy!" A second sled was on the run about a hundred and fifty yards behind them.

There was another straight stretch, and Jess estimated they entered the zig-zag curve at close to seventy-five miles an hour. On the zag of the turn, he understeered, and the sled went very high, catching the lip of the curve's top edge. It threw the sled back down into the course with a vengence, and this time they ricocheted off both walls. Snow and chewed ice flew off the run in great clouds and sprayed the riders with more grief.

"Nathan!" Jess called above the wind and the sled's clattering rumble.

"W-W-W-hat?" The little man's teeth were chattering from the fierce cold. The chill factor must have been well below zero.

"What's at the end of this thing? We're going to need a fast escape."

Nathan hollered back, "C-C-Cars, snowmobiles,

snow cat. What we need is a t-t-tank! Heated! At the r-r-rate we're going, we're not going t-to have to worry about it anyway!"

The sled screamed through another turn onto a steep straightaway. It continued to pick up even more speed.

Jess was better in the next half dozen curves. If the straight stretches were long enough, the men could hear the automatic weapons popping behind them. But none of the shots came close enough to be noticed.

The final mile of the course was their undoing—and probably their salvation. Try as he would, Jess was unable to keep the sled from going too high on the sculptured ice curves.

"Tom, I really think you ought to use those brakes! I don't do this every weekend!" The young giant was trying to make himself heard over the quiet roar of a slipstream that had to be at least ninety miles an hour.

Another curve loomed, Jess cut low, and the sled went high with undissipated speed. The ex-Marine was not braking. Out of the turn, the sled bounced back and forth between the icy walls several times before Jess could bring it under control. With an experienced pilot, there would be no braking, but an experienced pilot would also know what line to take through the sharp turns—and it would be daylight!

"Tom, what's going on back there?"

"Tom! Tom, wake up!"

Hanging on to the handrails for dear life, Nathan managed to turn around just in time to see the unconscious man come to life and try to figure out exactly where he was and what he was doing. The undersecretary of state's back had been cradled between the sled's rear braces that held the pusher handles. It was a miracle he hadn't toppled off.

Unknown to the four souls hurtling down the mountain at over ninety miles an hour, "Big Rocky," the curve that had claimed a half dozen lives over the years was next on the course. Jess knew the ex-Marine must have passed out again because as they went into the curve the brakes didn't grab, and there was no way the sled was going to stay on Mother Earth. This time, when the sled was thrown off the curve for going too fast, it hit the right wall hard enough to bounce it airborne. It flew off the course at eighty-five miles an hour, twisting in a series of quick barrel rolls. It clipped two pine trees, which managed to slow the rolling somewhat, and as it spiraled parallel to the mountain's slope for another forty yards, it finally came to earth, bouncing in the deep snow several times before the nose could hit and submerge once and for all. The men were thrown off the spinning sled at various places down the slope.

On the course, the Arabs, with their brakeman, managed to negotiate Big Rocky. However, they did not realize until they'd scraped to a stop at the end of a long rooster-tail spray of ice that there was no sled in front of them.

A mile up the mountain behind them, Jess made his way back up the slope to find the other men. Tom Oliver was the first to fall off the sled, and Jess struggled through the snow until he reached him. The young giant could see the other men getting up. It appeared no one was seriously hurt, but if something wasn't done, they might freeze to death.

Oliver was unconscious, his shirt soaked with blood. Jess knew they would never get off the mountain without being caught if they had to carry him. He quickly worked his miracle on the man before the others could reach them. The bullet had passed through the shoulder, and Jess healed the torn tissue and blood vessels and repaired the chipped bone in a matter of seconds. He left the entry and exit wounds not completely healed. He also speeded up the ex-Marine's metabolism to generate the necessary heat to keep him alive. When the other two men did arrive, hugging their shoulders in the international gesture of being cold, the undersecretary was sitting up and probing an itchy shoulder.

Jess was the first to speak. "He's okay. Let's get out of here."

"Are you sure?"

Oliver answered himself. "Yeah, believe it or not, I really feel fine—no pain. The bullet went through clean."

"Let me take a look, Tom." Derry stepped forward and was going to examine the wound.

"Forget it. Let's get out of here. There's not enough light to see anything anyway. I feel fine. Let's go!"

"Wait." Nathan was looking at his own bloody sleeve in stark horror. Jess looked at the little man and said, "Nathan, what happened?"

"The bullet must have gone through my arm after it left Tom. Either that or I caught another one. I never felt it. Now it's starting to hurt." Blood was dripping off the end of his hand at an alarming rate.

Derry looked at him in disbelief and said, "Let me see." The aide rolled up the sleeve of the little man, and, sure enough, there were holes where the bullet had entered and exited through the upper arm. Blood flowed freely from each.

"Wow! It's gonna hurt a lot more, too. We better put a tourniquet on it."

"Here, let me help." Jess took off his belt and got down on his knees to level the height. He wrapped the little man's arm and fastened the belt. By now the pain was throbbing, and Nathan was on the verge of fainting. He looked into the young man's face, searching, pleading, but said nothing.

Jess looked up from his work, smiled, and said, "It's done." Again he had performed the most wondrous of all miracles ever performed on earth save raising the dead. Nathan felt the pain immediately leave, and a tremendous rush of well-being flowed through him. As he did with Tom Oliver, Jess left the superficial wounds so that the other men would not suspect what had happened. Nathan reached with his good arm and grabbed Jess's arm as he was standing up. There were already tears in his eyes as he said, "Thanks, Jessie. I owe you one. Or two." The little man was slowly shaking his head and looking up at the giant in awe. The questions he was as yet unable to ask temporarily faded. He would find out later what Jess did to the sheikh—if anything.

Jess moved to Derry, casually touched him on the shoulder, and said, "We've got to get off this mountain—away from the run. They'll backtrack up the course when they don't find the sled." Not until the next day would the attorney wonder why he didn't feel the effects of wading through half a mile of snow in freezing temperatures. He would finally chalk it up to adrenaline.

They had moved out of the snow line and were following a cow path in an open field when Jess said casually, "Gentlemen, I think you may be happy to know that I liberated a souvenir from the sheikh's little hovel in order to keep you in the manner to which you've become accustomed. Eventually, Nathan, I expect you to send it back."

# 7

From his shirt pocket, inside his sweater, Jess pulled out a folded cellular phone and handed it to Nathan. "Surprise! Care to call a taxi and have it pick us up down there?" Below them the men could see the winding stream of streetlights on the main road that led into the town.

"Jess, I don't believe you. That's exactly what I'm going to do. You don't happen to know the number, do you?"

Jess replied in a perfect German accent, *"Weissberg Taxi ist fünf fünf fünf, ein sieben ein sieben."*

Nathan took the phone and said, "There's always gotta be one." He punched in 5-5-5–1-7-1-7, and the phone was a long time ringing. Holding it to his ear, he continued speaking. "The run ends on the other side of town. If we're lucky, our friends won't figure out what's happened until we're long gone. We'll let the taxi take us all the way to Bern. The jet can meet us there. It's going to hit the fan when Ali finds out what . . . Hello? *Sprechen Sie Englisch?*"

The plane arrived in Bern after the men had only waited half an hour. On board were an Air Force doctor and two nurses. They bandaged the wounds of the two men hit by gunfire, but the men didn't seem to be too concerned. There was no pain. The doctor was surprised the wounds were already healing so fast, but apparently the bullets had missed the bone and anything else that was vital. Both men would be x-rayed when they got back to the United States in about six hours.

The day after they returned, Nathan called Jess and asked him to make the trip to the NSA complex and the agent's office. He quizzed the young man thoroughly, but got nowhere.

"Nathan, I told you there could be a reaction. I don't have control over which way his brain decides to jump." Nathan had to take the boy's word for it. He did not dare, on a governmental scale, protest the sheikh's men trying to kill them. An investigation might reveal far too many things better kept under wraps. The sheikh's empire did not protest whatever it was the Americans obviously had done to their master because an investigation would reveal they'd tried to kill the Americans. Better to let all sleeping dogs lie.

It would be several months before the sheikh recovered his mental capacities. Until then, he was a raving maniac requiring around-the-clock care. When he finally did regain his senses, he was a different man. While insane, his mind shuffling slipshod around the inside of his head, he evidently came to the conclusion that he didn't like himself very much.

Two days later, Jess was back at his studies, and Dr. Fielder and his staff graduated the young giant into the realm of the body's skeletal structure. Jess began healing broken and diseased bones. The patients were already under anesthesia when he performed his miracles. It would never do for a construction worker with a compound fracture to watch the boy silently meld several pieces of shattered bone back together and then seal the skin wounds without even leaving a scar. Fielder made sure casts were put on broken bones and that patients were led to believe they would be fine in two or three months.

If the fracture was slight, the explanation for the miraculous recoveries was that the breaks couldn't have been all that serious to begin with. If there was bone disease—cancer, tumors, osteosclerosis—Jess put them on the slow schedule so that the miraculous cure wouldn't be linked to him.

Three weeks after Jess began on the body's skeleton, Nathan again showed up at six in the morning.

"Jess, we've got another problem I think you can help us with."

"That's what you're paying me for, Nathan. What can I do?"

"The president is sending Senator Lee Hong, from

New York, to Rotterdam to work on a trade agreement with the Chinese during the European Summit this week. The Chinese have been invited to participate as associate partners, and in return they are going to release several dozen political prisoners and dissolve tariffs on foreign grain imports. This will mean a windfall for our U.S. farmers. The senator is an American of Chinese descent. Probably no one else would be able to pull off what he's doing; he knows them, he speaks their language."

"What's wrong with him?"

Nathan's face showed a miniscule smile as he said, "He was playing baseball with his kids in his front yard and tore some ligaments in his groin while demonstrating a hook slide into second base. He's on crutches and in a great deal of pain unless he's taking painkillers. The doctors have tried several, and he seems to have a reaction to most of them. The ones he doesn't react to dull his senses so badly he's rendered next to useless. We'd really like him in Class A shape."

"Nathan, let's be honest with each other. When we came back from Switzerland, I asked a lot of questions about your friend Ali. He wasn't what you told me at all. He was some of the things you said he was, but he's also an international terrorist. He sells arms to both sides; he sells classified information to anybody who will pay. To this day I don't know why you'd want to keep a man like that alive.

What's the senator's real purpose with the Chinese? Don't snow me, I can take it."

The NSA man was noticeably taken aback.

"Who did you talk to about Ali?"

"It's common knowledge, Nathan. What I resent is your trying to treat me like a kid who can't take the truth about these men and the way our government does business. You forget my father was in the middle of all that stuff for over twenty years. I don't trust anybody. I don't believe anything I hear until I can prove it. I don't even believe what my eyes show me because I know how effective the magician's illusions can be. Now, what's the real reason you want me to fix Hong?"

"Jess, I don't see that as any of your business. You're being well paid to use your ability. There are some things it's better that you don't know. I'll give you this, though; I won't make up any more stories. I'll just ask you to do it. How's that?"

Jess knew that he'd find out everything about Hong, and anybody else, when he touched them anyway, so he simply said, "That's better than your lying to me."

"If it helps any, I can give you this—Ali was blackmailing us. We needed to keep him alive long enough to find what we were looking for."

"And he's your good friend."

"That's the way it works in government. We all act friendly while we watch our backs for sharp objects."

"Why don't you try looking at the Transworld Shipping, warehouse number six on pier two in Singapore. If they haven't been moved, you'll find the nuclear fuses in some boxes in the annex. They're labled 'Archeological Stuffs—Alexandria Historical Society, Alexandria, Egypt'. You'd better get them before Hussad gets them."

Nathan was stupefied. He cried, "How do you know this?"

"I have my sources—quote, end of quote."

"Sources? You gotta be kidding. Can you read minds too?"

"Nathan, I overheard two of the men at his home. They didn't know I was there. I remembered enough of the words to look them up in the Arabic dictionary in the sheikh's library. A lot of the words sound the same in English—*Transworld Warehouse, Alexandria*—you get the picture."

"I can't believe this. You may have helped us way beyond what you could possibly imagine."

"Just tell me the truth from now on."

"You got a deal."

That night Jess met the Chinese-American senator from New York. The next morning the senator could not believe that the pain he'd been suffering was gone.

The next week Nathan was taken to the White House and ushered into the president's private quarters at seven in the morning. Even at that hour the president's slick black hair was in perfect form, and his piercing blue eyes were as penetrating as they appeared on national TV. Between furious sneezes, a horrible cellar-deep cough, and two trips to the john with diarrhea, he apologized three times for the inconvenience of asking Jess to use his gift for such a trivial reason—the common flu, for which he had been inoculated. He was due on Capitol Hill at nine to give an address and initiate a bitter debate over, of all things, credit cards. Congress had refused to help, so the president was initiating legislation to limit the gluttonous interest banks were allowed to charge on credit cards, in addition to all the add-ons—yearly fees, late charges, and fees charged to the stores and businesses that take the cards. Several times Jess had heard the president say on national TV that the greed of America's banks was eating up the paychecks of the middle class—the middle class that had elected him on his promise that he would take things out on the rich for a change and give the average citizen a break.

America's number one citizen went to the Hill that morning without so much as a sniffle. Later that day Jess was called to the phone.

"Mr. Waterson?"

"Yes."

"Please hold one moment for the president of the United States."

Jess was more than a little surprised.

The familiar voice broke the twenty seconds of silence. "Jess?"

"Yes, sir."

"You did a dandy job, my boy. I can't thank you enough."

"I'm glad you're feeling better, Mr. President."

"Listen, when was the last time you had any time off?"

"I'd have to think. It's been a while."

"Well, I want you to take a couple of weeks with pay. Nathan said you have been hard at it for a long time now. All work and no play, you know."

"Thank you, sir. I may do that. My mom has been on my case lately for just that."

"Take a couple—enjoy yourself. I'll make sure Nathan works it out with Dr. Fielder."

"Thank you again, sir."

That afternoon Jess packed his Cherokee with a suitcase of fall clothes and his mountain bike. The next morning, before dawn, he was on the road north. He had no particular destination. By the middle of the afternoon, he was in the heart of the largest park in the lower forty-eight and a most spectacular display of fall colors. The Adirondack Park fills most of the top half of the state of New York and includes over thirteen thousand square miles of woods, lakes, and rivers. Though much of the land is private and includes scores of towns, the park has one of the most pristine wilderness areas in the United States. In places, a hiker can walk twenty-five miles and not hit a main road.

The vacancy sign flashing in front of the Racquette Lodge drew him like a magnet, and once inside the lobby he found himself surrounded by rustic log walls decorated with dozens of mounted trophy fish representing a number of species.

"Best place is across the bridge on the right."

Everything was in walking distance, and while he was walking to the restaurant the clerk recommended for supper, Jess noticed the blue and yellow state marker next to the bridge.

"Racquette Lake, source of the Racquette River, the most extensively harnessed river in the world." The sign went on to explain that because of a drop of over fourteen hundred feet in the seventy miles to where it emptied into the St. Lawrence, there were more dams and powerhouses per mile than on any other waterway in the world.

The next morning Jess headed out of town on his bike. The air snapped with the smells of autumn. Temperature was in the high sixties. The concentrated smell of wood whacked him in the nose as he passed several sawmills. It was an exhilarating smell, perfectly complementing the bouquet of thousands of pine, spruce, and fir trees on either side of the Adirondack Road. He got into the woods a couple of times on trails, but the paths quickly brought him back to the blacktop. The road itself was an endless theme and variations on hills. There were very few flat stretches. Jess welcomed the exertion.

A little after eleven he had just climbed a mile-long stretch bordered by hardwoods. He couldn't seem

to get enough of the fresh-musty smell of the leaves.
At the top of the hill there was a little red MG pulled
onto the shoulder. The right rear tire was flat.

"Hey." He stopped the bike and got off. She was
leaning against the car, arms folded in frustration.

"Hi."

And she was stunning.

"Looks like a serious case of *flatus tireus*."

The incredible smile hit Jess like a concussion
grenade. The next thing out of his mouth was rather
stupid. "Did anyone ever tell you that you look a lot
like Barbara Hershey—before her lip job?"

"No. No one ever has." She smiled again. This
time it shot across her eyes and down her face in
surprised amusement. The effect again sent the
young giant's mind tumbling.

"You know who she is?" Head nodding in abject
sincerity, Jess knew he'd already got behind the
power curve.

"Yes. I just saw *Beaches* for the third time last
week."

She had the thickest hair—rich, chicory brown. It
curled and splashed across her shoulders with red
highlights glistening whenever she turned her head.
A teal ribbon exactly matched teal eyes—Barbara
Hershey's are brown.

Bedroom eyes some would call them, the lids
dropped seductively perhaps a sixteenth of an inch
lower than decency allows. Dark amber eye shadow
dissolved outwardly to a pastel gold. Her eyebrows

were thick and natural—meticulously elongated commas. Her nose—flawlessly sculptured as if an artist had designed it. With such thick hair, Jess guessed she might have a mustache that had been waxed off. If anything, her lips were a little on the thin side—exactly why Barbara had decided to get the collagen job. Jess could see a tiny scar on her forehead, and her whole face was perhaps a quarter of an inch too long for its width. Had it been perfectly proportioned, she would have looked like a china doll—artificial, unreal. She was tall, at least five-ten. All the bumps and curves were in the exact required proportions, and she looked like she was in excellent shape. She was wearing stone-washed jeans, Nike running shoes, and over a plain white blouse she wore a navy blue cardigan sweater with dozens of appliquéd shields and crests. The bottom line was she was one of the most beautiful and understated women Jess had ever seen.

"That was after the lip surgery. I liked her better before."

"She's a beautiful woman either way." Her voice was a little guarded.

"I rest my case." The young giant was blushing hotly.

To ease his embarrassment, she switched the detoured conversation back onto the main road and said, "I could change this, but I don't have a jack. I think I'll need a wrecker."

Jess gave her a half grin and said, "You'll think I'm showing off."

"Pardon?"

He continued, "Well, I could go back to town and get a wrecker—if they've got one. It'd take the best part of two hours." Her face fell considerably.

His grin went to three-quarter-face as he said, "Or you could lift the car up and I'll change the tire."

Jess was pleasantly surprised when she didn't come back with the predictable, "Oh sure, that'll be the day!" or its variations. Instead, she matched his grin and said, "Or . . ."

"Or . . . Wonder Boy, Jess Waterson, could lift the car up while you change the nasty thing. But I already told you—you'll think I'm showing off."

Her smile funneled into an open mouth as she said, "You can't lift this car—not even enough to . . . long enough to . . . you can't . . ."

Jess continued to grin.

"No way!"

"Open the trunk. Let's get the spare. You sure you know how to do this?"

"I do this every Monday, Wednesday, and Friday between the hours of two and four. I find a good back road, then I stop, get out, stick a nail in the tire and then I just have right at it!" She was flirting with Jess, and he liked it—a lot! "But I gotta see to believe any part of this act." Her jaw was now dropped in a Melanie Griffith "I-just-swallowed-the-bird" cat grin.

Jess leaned the spare up against the little car next to the flat's wheel well. "Emergency brake on?"

"Yup."

"Iron." He put out his hand like a surgeon requiring an instrument. She had been standing hip-shot, wielding the tire iron loosely like a rag doll. She slapped it in his hand. Jess refused the pain and loosened the lug nuts on the wheel. Standing, he handed the iron back.

Locking his fingers and turning his hands inside out to produce a flurry of pops and cracks, he said, "Do you want the one-hand lift or the two?"

"Get real! I don't believe you can do it with both . . . and both feet . . . and your father . . . and all your uncles . . ."

Her grin and kidding tirade stopped in midsentence when Jess reached down, grabbed the back bumper with one hand, and yanked the little car's whole rear end two feet into the air.

The Melanie Griffith grin froze in astonishment.

"You going to stand there? Or are you going to change the tire?"

She broke out of the shock and quickly and efficiently went to work, glancing at the boy every chance she could. He wasn't even sweating—yet. It didn't take long. He switched hands, then went to both hands. Jess couldn't see over the fender to tell how she was progressing, and he was beginning to get tired.

"How're you doing down there?"

"Oh, the wheezy-mecallit doesn't want to slide onto the bachadookie."

"What?" The bumper was cutting into his hands. Carefully crossing over, he turned around with his back to the car so he could use his legs as leverage. Now he really couldn't see what was going on.

"Listen, Moose, I need to take a little break here. I think I'm a little faint—probably the heat. Don't let it down, whatever you do! I still don't have the darn spare on."

"Wait a minute!" Now the pain in the young boy's hands was getting serious.

She stood up, reached into the back seat, and pulled out a beach towel.

"Oh, my, my. These things do tire, I said tire, me out so." Jess turned his head as far as he could to see what she was up to. She was doing an imitation of Scarlett O'Hara, waving the towel in front of her face in a fanning motion.

"Wait a minute. There're no timeouts allowed here. I'm in serious . . . pain—a—"

"I just think li'l ol' me is going to faint." She faked it, catching herself on the side of the car. Then, abruptly, she tumbled inside, legs lazily propped on the convertible's door.

By now the pain was into the unbearable stage, and against his will, Jess dropped the little car to the ground.

"Oh, de-ah." Still Scarlett.

He stepped to the side of the car, aching, rubbing

his hands, and was shocked to see that the spare was on as if it had been born there. It then dawned on him that it had been on for several minutes. She'd changed it in record time, then let him hang out to dry.

"You . . ."

He now got the full-face grin, and once more the effect was stunning.

Sheepishly, he shook his head. Had!

"Cruel. Cruel. Enough to give a growing boy a hernia." More Scarlett.

"It probably came close!" Jess recovered quickly. He continued, "Are you going to tell me your name?" She opened the door and got out of the car.

"Lottie. Beringer. You're Jess Waterson, Wonder Boy extraordinaire." She had been wiping her hands on the towel and reached out to shake the young giant's hand. The smile just would not let up on him.

"You're quite a bale of cotton, Lottie Beringer. I feel like the boat that's just splattered all over the rocks, lured there by Lorelei." He was still shaking his arms, trying to get the circulation going again.

"Oh, it's not that bad. I had fun. Tell you what, Wonder Boy. Are you into homemade vegetable soup and chicken salad with pineapple, et cetera, sandwiches on thick homemade bread?"

"That sounds heavenly. Your place or mine?"

"Mine. Strap the bike to the luggage rack. My mama always says, 'If you're gonna lure 'em onto the rocks, you gotta feed 'em.'"

For the twenty minutes it took her to negotiate the main road and several back roads, they pumped each other for the vitals. Lottie was three months older than Jess. She was a zoology major on her way to veterinarian school, and best of all, she was from a small town in western Maryland and a sophomore at the University of Maryland—only an unbelievable ten minutes from where Jess worked! Her widowed grandmother was staying alone at the family's year-round cottage on Blue Mountain Lake when she took a bad fall. The elderly woman had spent two days in the hospital, then returned to the cottage. Lottie's parents were in Europe, and the young woman skipped classes for a couple of days to drive up and make sure her grandmother was all right.

After lunch, grandmother safely tucked in a comforter on the daybed in front of the picture window, Lottie took Jess down to the boathouse. He was pleasantly surprised to see an antique, varnished mahogany Chris Craft speedboat.

"That is magnificent!"

"This boat has been in our family for over forty years. Daddy has it refinished every couple of years. It's got all the original equipment—goes like a scared cat."

They rode for the better part of an hour. Jess saw little of the lake. He couldn't take his gaze off the teal eyes and flowing brown hair. When he took the wheel, he noticed she couldn't take her eyes off him either.

"Wanna ski?"

"It's almost October. That water's like ice!"

"Just don't fall, big boy. You'll be okay."

Jess was hesitant but wasn't about to let his manhood come under fire. If he took off sitting on the dock, came back, and released in shallow water, he could pull it off—he wouldn't even get wet.

They went back to the boathouse, and Lottie clipped the ski rope to the boat's ring. A pair of neon-swirled skis were standing in the corner. She turned to him and said, "You're not one of those wimps who needs two skis are you?"

"Give me a break!"

The old inboard gobbled and grumbled as she slowly pulled the line taut.

He hollered, "Hit it!" She firewalled the throttle, and he stood up to become instantly waterborn.

She let the young giant ski for about five minutes, getting his sea legs, gaining confidence as he sliced across the brittle fall water. She waited until he was maxed out on the outside of a turn, then she turned around to face him, gave him a dead-cat smile, and purposely turned the boat into his glide.

"Aaaaggghhhh!"

"Ooops!"

Jess desperately pulled the rope high over his head to take out the slack, but he never had a chance. Slowly, surely, he settled into the fifty-five-degree water up to his neck before the boat finally took up the slack and pulled him out of the hole. Grinning,

dripping, he shook his blue fist at her and shouted,
"You did that on purpose, Beringer! Yours is coming!"

The Melanie Griffith grin was back.

Soaking and freezing, he let the rope go as she
came by the boathouse. He coasted to a stop in about
a foot of water, sand bottom. Lottie brought the
boat back to the dock that ran alongside the boathouse. Jess caught it and tied it up.

"Looks like you zigged when you should have
zagged, Wonder Boy."

"Setup! You pulled the oldest dump in the world.
I watched the whole thing as I slowly sank into the
freezer."

"I would not stoop to something that mean.
Surely you jest, sir." It was Scarlett again—in all her
finery.

They had walked about half the length of the
dock's thirty feet when Jess very conveniently
tripped over a rope.

"Watch it!"

"Whooopsss!"

He managed to knock her into the water and
tumbled in after her.

"Yeeeeooooowwwww, this is cold!"

"Even! Even Steven, Ice Woman!"

"Touché!"

They were both laughing so hard it was all they
could do to wade to the shore to get out of the icy
water.

Grandmother had been watching when Lottie dumped Jess. She'd also seen him knock her into the lake. She had robes and thick beach towels waiting at the door.

"Scoot! Get out of those things. You'll both come down with pneumonia. At your ages!"

Jess's wet clothes went into the dryer. After supper, Mrs. Beringer insisted that Lottie take him back to the motel in Racquette Lake to get his things and check out. He would stay with them for the next two days, which were Saturday and Sunday. There was plenty of work to be done around the place to prepare for winter. Lottie's first class wasn't until one o'clock Monday afternoon. If she left early Monday morning, she could have all day Sunday. It was about a seven-hour drive.

Weather-wise, the next two days were Xerox copies of Friday—clear blue skies with cotton clouds, temperatures in the high sixties. Lottie's grandmother kept them busy painting, cleaning, buttoning up, preparing the cottage for the merciless winter ahead. The place was heated and insulated and could be used during the winter, but it rarely was.

What she could not do was prevent the horseplay. The pranks never let up, each an attempt to top the last. One time she looked out the front window to find the couple Indian leg-wrestling on the front lawn. Lottie caught Jess just right and turned the young giant in a backward somersault.

In his whole life, Jess had never been so happy and content. He had never had so much pure, unadulterated fun. At times, he sensed strongly that Lottie was trying desperately to hold back. He knew there was no boyfriend and couldn't imagine why. Other times, overwhelmed by the incredible chemistry, she let go, and it was as if they had been together for a lifetime.

It wasn't until Sunday night that Jess tried to kiss her.

She came into his arms easily. They were standing at the end of the dock watching the northern lights do their thing—a little early in the season. Elfin spirals of steam levitated over the lake, at odds with the crisp fall air. When he turned her face up to his and kissed her, she allowed it for a few seconds, then slowly pulled away.

"Jess, you don't know me. We can't do this. There are some things you don't know." He sensed she was on the verge of tears. Had he chosen to, he could have read her mind. However, it would be a despicable and ludicrous thing to do—like watching someone in the bathroom through the keyhole.

"You're not married."

"No, of course not."

"You don't have a boyfriend."

"No."

"Well?"

Lottie reached deep inside for the strength to tell him what was growing inside her, but there was just not enough strength in her to do it. She wanted him more than she wanted life itself. The end result was that she said nothing, and when he once more tried to kiss her, she abandoned all restraint and fell into the deep black hole.

# 8

Lottie had seven hours to consider how to tell Jess about her problem. She went through scheme after scheme, usually ending up in tears. How had it happened? "Why me?" Things were complicated enough without meeting Jess and falling helplessly in love. Even at nineteen it was possible to know for sure that there would never be another man—another opportunity like this! He completed and fulfilled her. In two days she had found out that she had been living as only half a person. With him, each day—each hour—had been better than the one before, and that phenomenon comes only once in a lifetime to a very lucky few.

To tell him would undoubtedly drive him away, and never to see him again . . . How was she going to tell him and not lose him?

The next two days of Jess's vacation were a bore. He no longer had any interest in the mountains. He made the trip back to Virginia and went boat shopping. With all the money he had in the bank, Jess had never indulged himself. He lived with his folks, he had no extravagant habits, he often gave money to people and organizations that needed it, but other than necessities, he'd never spent any on himself. The memories of Lottie in the boat were precious. His own family had spent a lot of time on the water over the years.

He might have bought a sailboat, but his mind was quickly made up for him the first time he laid eyes on the forty-two-foot boat of his dreams—a Cigarette—at a dealership in Annapolis. With two five-hundred-horse engines, it would do over eighty. It was expensive, but he was helpless. Besides, an eighteen-year-old in a sailboat blistering the water at speeds up to eighty miles an hour?

The dealer gave him several hours of instruction on the water, and Jess spent two days tearing up and down the bay scaring the seagulls. It was unbelievably exhilarating, and he couldn't wait to get Lottie on board. Each night he called her and they talked for at least an hour, but he was saving the boat as a surprise. Each time she seemed warm but, surprisingly, a little distant. She put him off when he asked her out for Friday night but finally agreed to let him pick her up Saturday morning so they could spend part of the day together. Jess didn't tell her where they were going. When she came into the lounge of the sorority house and saw him standing there, blond curls almost in the chandelier, she melted, and before she could stop, she was in his arms.

The boat was a wonderful surprise, and at times Lottie forgot herself and it was as though everything were normal. Standing in bolster seats at seventy miles an hour, she clung to his arm, her heart racing as fast as the engines. It was as if he were the start and end of her world—she needed nothing else. Then the darkness descended and she pushed herself away.

For Jess, she was there with him. That was all he needed.

At four o'clock Lottie knew she should go, but her attempts to get him to take her back were, at best, feeble. After getting tired of jouncing around, Jess looked for a secluded cove or backbay. There didn't seem to be any on their side of the bay. He didn't want to cross the several miles of open water to get to the Eastern Shore—it was too late in the day. Coming back across open water in the dark would be dangerous. He settled for anchoring a few hundred yards off the shoreline near Shady Side.

Jess had stocked the refrigerator and cupboards with enough food for the entire weekend. The couple ate tons of crab legs and fried clams reheated in the microwave; potato salad, cheese curd, cucumber cream cheese on bagel chips; and a number of other chewies, crunchies, and munchies. They talked and the hours flew by. Jess had a pile of cassettes for the stereo system. Background music ran the gamut of everything from Strauss to Paul Simon to Bill Monroe.

Lottie had almost worked up the nerve to tell him she was two months pregnant when Jess kissed her. Again she tumbled into the confusion of the conflict between not leading him on and the world-shaking necessity of his love. The talk turned to sex.

*Well, looks like now it's going to come out, like it or not.*

Lying in his arms, Lottie wanted him more than anything she'd ever wanted in her life, but she was totally flabbergasted when he told her he was a virgin and to him sex before marriage was wrong.

"I didn't think there were any left. I thought virgins were an extinct species."

"That choice has always been an integral part of my life. Does it disappoint you, Lottie?"

"No. In fact, it makes me love you all the more."

"Love? You said love . . . ?"

"Jess, there's something I've . . ."

She never got to finish the sentence.

When Jess anchored the boat, it was daylight. There were no other boats in sight. It had got dark and the anchor light had never been turned on. He certainly didn't realize that Hanky Baker was making his third drug run for the week up the Chesapeake Bay in his hundred-mile-an-hour Apache. Hanky had the radar on to watch for other boats, but Jess's low-profile Cigarette didn't show up. With the evening chop and his involvement with Lottie, Jess wasn't even listening for other boats.

Going over ninety, Hanky cut Jess's Cigarette cleanly in half and went airborne in the explosion of his right-side gas tank. Before Jess could even say, "What—" the two sections of his boat were on their way to the bottom of Chesapeake Bay with the couple still on the V-berth.

The cold water hit them like a sledgehammer. The only tiny bit of good fortune to make up for the unbelievably bad luck of getting hit in hundreds of square miles of open water was that the bow was pointing downward. Otherwise, they could easily have been trapped. Jess grabbed Lottie's arm and instinctively swam toward the cockpit hatch. There was only open water as the front half of the boat dropped away on its journey to the bottom. Jess struggled toward what he hoped was the surface. In the pitch-black darkness, it was impossible to tell.

Lottie was limp. She had been closest to the crash. Jess had been bounced very hard, was sore in a dozen places, and was still in shock. He swam only on instinct. Mercifully, he broke the surface after only ten feet and trod water. He quickly found that she wasn't breathing, and his mind exploded with stark horror. The young giant panicked, and prying her mouth open without even a good seal, he pumped terror-stricken breaths down her throat as fast as he could to force her to breathe. The slipshod mouth-to-mouth worked, and his heart began beating again only when she coughed and started, once more, to breathe slowly, irregularly. He probed as best he could to find out what was wrong with her, but his power had been short-circuited by the shock.

"Lottie! . . . Lottie!"

He tried desperately to bring her to, using his miraculous gift, but too many other stimuli were bombarding the brain, chief of which were the freezing water and the lights on the shoreline showing that civilization was a very long way off.

Jess took her in a cross-chest carry and started for the shore. He was already tired. Hanky Baker's boat was nowhere to be seen. Unknown to Jess, it was resting on the bottom over a hundred feet below him. Hanky had gone down with his load.

The lights refused to get closer. If anything they seemed farther away. Maybe he was drifting in the bay current. He closed his eyes and pulled, stroke after stroke, opening his eyes only to make sure he was headed toward the shore. Once, he found to his horror that he wasn't. The young giant's tremendous muscles bitterly rebelled at the trauma of the crash and the unrelenting temperature of the water. It never occurred to him to let Lottie go and swim for it on his own.

"Pull, fool . . . Pull . . . Stroke."

The fatigue got worse . . . and worse . . . and worse. Jess could barely lift his arms. Man was not designed to swim in water this incredibly cold. He'd float for a minute, then take a couple dozen strokes, sure that the current was negating all his effort.

"What difference does it make?"

He gave up twice. Each time, a tiny something deep inside gave him the strength to take one more stroke. Three times he went under with his burden. The chop of the waves harangued him, filling his mouth, making him cough, choke. Lottie never stirred. When he finally gave up, content to drift into the welcome sleep beneath the waves, he was too far gone to feel the arms around him, lifting, separating him from his burden. He barely heard the voices of the cutter's coasties, who had seen the explosion of Hanky's boat from three miles up the Bay and had rushed wide-open-throttle to search frantically for survivors of what had to be a super collision. Only by chance had they spotted Jess. Another five seconds, and he and Lottie would have made a watery exit to the next world. The boy's strength had simply run out.

He became remotely aware of voices, white, lights, more white, the smell of alcohol, and other infirmary affronts. Vaguely, he felt the helicopter lift off the cutter's deck and head toward Annapolis Memorial. When he finally regained full consciousness, a nurse was adjusting a bag of intravenous glucose. A special electric blanket was gradually bringing his body temperature from the high eighties back to the high nineties.

"Lottie! Where is she?"

"She's okay. She's in a room down the hall."

"She's alive?"

"Alive, conscious, and recovering nicely. I can't say the same for the baby though."

"Baby?"

"She had a miscarriage, son. She lost the baby."

"The *baby*?"

"Yes, she was two months. You knew that."

Jess's brain wouldn't assimilate the bizarre information, and he immediately fell asleep.

When he awoke the next time, his mother was sitting next to him.

"Hey, Sailor."

"Hi, Mom."

Jess didn't feel like talking to anyone but Lottie. He had to know what was going on. The nurse had obviously mistaken Lottie for another woman on the ward.

"Your father's on the way. He was in Richmond."

"I'm okay, Mom. How is Lottie?" Jess had told his folks about Lottie—in glowing detail, but they had not met her yet.

"She's okay, Jess. I met her a while ago. We had a long talk. She's one of a kind, Jess. You're a lucky fellow."

"Mom, the nurse said she had a miscarriage. Lottie wasn't pregnant. The nurse was mixed up."

"Lottie said she tried and tried to tell you. She just hadn't been able to bring herself to do it yet."

"She was pregnant?"

"Yes, Jess, but . . ."

"NO! I don't want to hear it!"

"Jess, wait! You've got to talk to her! It isn't . . ."

"*NO! NO NO NO NO!*" His screams brought the nurse.

"It's okay. He's just upset." Stephanie knew there would be no getting through to him. He had submerged his mind in a way that only Jess could do. It would surface again when it could cope.

"It's best we leave him. He's going to have to sort through this on his own."

Jess only vaguely remembered his father coming into the room. Since it was well past midnight and the boy was out of danger, the Watersons left for home. They would return in the morning. When they did, Jess had already checked himself out. He had not gone to see Lottie. He took a taxi to where he'd left the Cherokee and drove straight to Walter Reed.

"Dr. Fielder, I'm resigning as of now."

"But Jess . . ."

The young giant dropped the written resignation on the desk and stormed out of the office with a flurry of protests darting his back. He refused to answer any questions; he refused even to say goodbye. They had a thousand times more data than they needed. He had known for some time that they were only keeping him busy so they could have access to his ability for their own purposes. He drove home, packed the suitcase again with fall clothes, left a note for his folks, and pointed the Jeep south.

When Fielder called Nathan Bartholomew and

told him Jess had resigned, the NSA agent went through the ceiling. He immediately set wheels turning to put his marked ace back in the deck. Nathan had not yet begun to tap the boy's talents, and the little bulldog from Brooklyn was not going to be denied.

Jess drove cross-country through Virginia until he hit I-64 at Charlottesville. He took it to I-81 and turned south. At about two in the afternoon he went through Roanoke. He crossed into Tennessee, and about an hour before dark, he got off the interstate and headed north toward Cherokee Lake. Avoiding any place that would have people, he finally found a dirt road that led to the water. He pulled the Jeep onto a grassy hillock, got out, and tried to decide what to do. He had driven all day in a fog. Except for what was needed to drive, his mental processes had been shut down in defense against the hurting. A burning barn was in his chest and he couldn't put it out. Once reality began to return, everywhere he looked there were memories of Lottie. Twice he'd seen red MGs, and twice he'd skidded into tailspins of additional pain. How could she have . . . ? How could she have possibly . . . ?

"All right, Waterson, grab yourself by the seat of the pants and yank! It ain't the end of the world." He'd been sitting leaned up against a large oak tree about a hundred feet from the lake's shoreline. Darkness had sunk into the woods and filled all the empty places. The lights from civilization winked at him from the other side of the lake. Somehow he had to force his mental faculties back into operation.

He wasn't sure whether Nathan would try to stop him or not. He was still officially on vacation, but he was going to go on the assumption that someone would be looking for him—hard! Leaving his folks that way bothered him too. However, he knew he could handle them. They had long ago grown accustomed to his independence. He would call them often. For the present, he must make it as hard as possible for the powers that be to find him. Maybe Uncle Colin and Aunt Marie in Nashville would have some advice.

Colin Hobkirk was retired FBI. He and Jess's father had gone through college together and had even worked together for the government on occasion. Colin had spent many nights at the Waterson home when he was working for the FBI and made once-a-month trips to D.C. Jess called the Hobkirks from a rest stop on I-40 just outside Cookeville. A small river flowed at the bottom of the hill. Jess followed a path and squatted on the bank. The brief thought darted through his mind: *I wish I could jump in and dissolve in the water. I could drift with the currents until I finally reached the sea, then make a decision about life.*

Marie answered the phone, said Colin was fishing, to come on and stay with them or face a fate worse than death.

"I'm somewhere west of Knoxville, Aunt Marie. I'll be there by suppertime."

Jess came within a hundred feet of making it. As he pulled up to the driveway and started to turn in, a brown van cut him off. Four men in suits got out quickly, identified themselves as NSA agents, and told him that if he did not come with them peacefully they would handcuff him.

"At least let me tell my aunt and uncle that I'm not going to stay with them."

"Sorry, we have strict orders."

Had Jess known what was in store for him, he would have tried to overpower them and escape. One of them drove off in the Cherokee to some unknown destination, and Jess was escorted to Tune Airport where an NSA Lear was waiting. In less than an hour and a half they were on the ground at Andrews, and the young giant was on his way to a place he would grow to hate over the next few months. He would find out later that Nathan had tapped the Hobkirks' phone—a gross violation of the law and interagency etiquette, even if Colin was retired.

They drove, by van again, for about an hour and a half. Jess felt they were going west, but it was dark out, and he couldn't sense the direction for sure. He remained seated on a bench in the back of the van. There were two men with him. One reason he did not try to escape was that he was curious as to just how far they would go. The van slowed for the last time, and Jess heard the jingling of a chain-link gate opening. The driver had been on the cellular phone for the last five minutes. The engine strained up a long, steep drive, and the van stopped beneath a portico. Jess was escorted into what appeared to be a large sitting room and told to wait. The two men stayed with him.

Twenty minutes later the helicopter landed bringing Nathan.

"Jess."

"Nathan."

"We need to talk."

"You need to talk, Nathan. I don't have much to say."

"You broke a contract."

"Nathan, Uncle Sam's in the business of breaking contracts. Consider the American Indian. Somehow I guessed you'd survive without me. Perhaps I was wrong. Uncle Sammy's obviously ground to a halt or I wouldn't be here."

"Jessie, I need your services. You're too valuable for me to let you get away. That's the long and short of it. I know about Lottie. I talked with your mom and dad. I think you should have heard it from her, but I'll save her the trouble and tell you myself. You know that Lottie wa . . ."

"SHUT UP ABOUT LOTTIE! You say one more word, and I'll plaster the blood of your goons here all over the walls!"

"Have it your way. It's out of my hands. The

president is pulling the strings now. He will offer you whatever you want, within reason, and you will do your little trick. If you do as we ask, you will be given access to the tutors and the computers again. If you don't, we'll just lock you up and forget about you."

"It's called kidnapping, Nathan. This is the United States of America. My dad will recognize your stonewalling and go to the media."

"And the media will cooperate with us, or they will suffer a giant dose of everything from the IRS to the FBI to the CIA to the NAACP, the OEO, the building codes department, and a host of other little goodies we have in our bag. When the president orders it, and they know it isn't just politics, be they Democrats or Republicans, whether they hate him or not, they follow orders just like everybody else. Believe it! We've done it all before."

"Then you'd better show me to my cell, Nathan. I could use a good rest anyway. The first person you force me to heal will get his mind blown the way your friend the sheikh did. You want to deal with that again?"

"So you did do it on purpose!"

"And I'll do it again."

"You may have cost Beckerman his life, kid!"

"He knew the risks."

Nathan left it at that. Jess was too depressed to entertain ways to overpower the men and escape. Later maybe. He was escorted to a small suite of rooms. There was a small sitting room about ten by twelve in which there was an overstuffed chair, a lamp, and an empty magazine rack. In the bottom of the magazine rack were a dozen hollow flies and two live spiders. An archway led into a small hall where doors opened to a bedroom and a small bathroom with a shower stall. There were no pictures on the walls and no carpets on the floor. Somebody definitely did not want the place to look like home. The only door in and out was solid steel. There were no windows, and Jess suspected that the walls were substantially more than just painted sheetrock. He heard the helicopter take off and had never felt more alone or depressed in his life.

They left him by himself for a whole month. The steel door would open, a man in a suit would bring his meals while another held the door. There was always a third man standing next to him. They weren't taking any chances. Jess occupied his time by reviewing as much of his learning in as many fields as he could remember. The solitude did not bother him anywhere near as much as they thought it would. He counted off the days by marking the sitting-room wall with the edge of his sneaker sole. The floor was dirty enough so that the sneaker would make a dark mark on the white paint. The biggest problem was keeping Lottie out of his mind. Every time she came around, he pushed her out with a gruff vengeance.

Stephanie and Jeff Waterson had been told nothing. When Jess didn't show for supper, Marie Hobkirk called Stephanie. Unfortunately, there had been no witnesses to see the van and the boy's abduction. Forty-eight hours later, Jeff filed a missing persons report with only half a heart. He strongly suspected that Bartholomew was behind it all, and in a way, that was a relief—at least the boy was safe. However, it was a constant source of frustration. The dozens of times Jeff called Nathan, the little man denied any knowledge of Jess. He feigned concern, said he would use his pull with local and Tennessee authorities, but nothing ever came of it.

The day Jess made his thirtieth mark on the wall, Nathan came to visit him.

"Well?" At least Nathan didn't mince words.

"I think I'd like a couple more months to think it over."

"Think about this. You owed us nine months on your contract. You've screwed around for one. That means you still owe us nine—I'll give you the one, and we'll call it eight left. Finish working for us those eight months, and we'll call it quits."

"Nathan, I would believe the pope needs a Wassermann before I'd believe any deal you offered me. You will keep me until the end of time or until you don't need me any more."

"If you believe that, why don't you make it easy on yourself. You know the routine—work, reward. It's that simple."

"Give me a couple of months. Then why don't you have your girl call my girl? Maybe we can do lunch."

The next thirty days went by as slowly as a truckload of molasses pouring down an Arctic hill. Jess grew sick of the mind games, and his hosts did not give him so much as a pencil. The only break from the boredom was exercising—jumping jacks, push-ups, running the few short strides from room to room—and it was all quickly growing old. Finally, when he decided it was time to see if anybody was out there besides the meal crew, he painted the walls of the sitting room with the lamp, the chair, the magazine rack, and the dresser. In spite of the incredible ruckus, nothing happened. It only confirmed that they had him on "Candid Camera" and didn't even have to open the door to see what was going on. All he accomplished was depriving himself of a place to sit. He tried ripping out the sink and shower stall in the bathroom but found that they had been specially bolted down. Someone had done his homework. No telling how many prisoners had been guests before.

For the next three days, every time he passed the steel door, he gave it a kick. After hundreds of kicks, the door was unscathed, he'd had to heal his swollen leg and foot several times, and he came to the conclusion that the door-kicking contest wasn't such a good idea either. After another three days, he picked up the splintered wood and chair stuffing he'd been walking over and dumped them in a corner. Then he picked it all up and carried it to another corner. Then he carried it into the bedroom and fit as much as he could into the dresser. Then he took it all back to the sitting room and split it into even piles, one for each corner. When there were almost ninety sneaker marks on the white paint, Jess could take it no longer.

"Okay, you win. Get Bartholomew." He was speaking to where he suspected one of the fiber optic camera lenses was hidden.

Five minutes later a suited man brought him a pile of magazines and a Craig Thomas paperback thriller. The next day Jess was brought downstairs for the first time in over three months. Nathan was waiting for him. Nathan didn't bother with the amenities.

"There's an African diplomat who's got AIDS. If he dies, so does the chance to stop the bloodbath in his country. They average thirty-five killings a day, and he's within an arm's length of getting the two sides together."

"Is this the truth, Nathan? Remember, we had a deal about your making up stories."

"This is the truth. The president wants him to live."

"And this 'healing' will open up the guy's country to American sharks in big industry."

"Something like that, yes."

"All right, if I fix him, where do I spend the night?"

"Back here. In another suite, one that is considerably more confortable."

"Not good enough. How about my home?"

"You'll go home when we firmly believe you won't run and not a minute before. You prove to us, beyond a shadow of a doubt, that you're playing quality ball, and you'll see happy faces everywhere you look. We don't like this any more than you do. It ties up good men who could be used on at least a dozen other projects."

"All right. Where's the African? You want me to do it by just shaking hands like before?"

"Any way you can. He'll be pointed out to you at a cocktail party at the state department tonight."

"Black tie?"

"Not for you. You'll be part of the kitchen staff. How you work it is up to you. I'll add this tiny bit of incentive: If you don't work it out, you get to spend the night in your old room. If you try to run, there'll be agents at every door, every window, every gate, even on the roof. I'm going to pull a whole battalion of them off some other details to make sure you stay put. If you blow that man's mind, you'll spend the rest of your life in Leavenworth, and you can take that to the bank!"

Jess healed the African by spilling a whole tray of drinks on him, then brushing him off with his hands. That night he was given new quarters that included a TV, a stereo, and, thank goodness, a computer hooked into the mainframe he had used at Walter Reed. He was also allowed to call his folks. Jeff and Stephanie were furious with the NSA for what they had done to Jess, but Jeff had been in government too long to believe he could make them pay.

"Steph, Jess will work it out. I have every faith in him that he'll make the piper pay and pay big."

Over the next three months, Nathan used the young giant's services a total of twelve times. Jess performed like a trained monkey, biding his time. They resumed the tutoring programs again, and he was also allowed to call home once a day. However, he remained confined to the mountain safe house. On Nathan's thirteenth healing project for Jess, the young giant confronted the little NSA man.

"Nathan, I want my freedom. I want to go home."

"When I feel we can trust you—not until."

"Trust me. I've done your bidding for three months now. What exactly do you think I'm going to pull?"

"You broke the contract, Jess. If you don't like the consequences, that's your problem."

"I'll bet you're still carrying grudges from grade school, Nathan."

Inside, Jess was fuming. There was no reason for them to keep him locked up other than Nathan's pathological need to control.

Two nights later Nathan sent the van for Jess. As usual, the boy was kept seated in the back, the front blocked off to prevent him from seeing out the windshield and identifying landmarks that would point to the location of the safe house. The young giant was still smoldering from Nathan's refusal to let him go home. They had no reason to treat him like a prisoner. An hour and fifteen minutes later, when the driver opened the door, they were under the White House portico.

"He's allergic to anything that will help him, Jessie. I realize this is beneath your talents again, but the country needs him healthy." Nathan remained professional. There was no warmth in his voice or his eyes.

Nathan told the doctor and nurse to take a break and go get some coffee before ushering Jess into the hallowed bedroom. The president was lying in bed, his nose bright red, his eyes bleary. Every few seconds he sneezed violently and then honked into a tissue.

Jess had expected a lot more from the president of the United States. He should have had enough gumption to work through a common cold. However, Jess had got the impression the last time he'd healed the man that Jeff Waterson was right—the president was America's number one hypochondriac. It was now obvious that the man was a milksop to boot.

"How are you doing, Mr. President?"

"It's about time! Why weren't you here earlier? I've been suffering since last night!"

"Sorry, sir. I was on safari in Africa. Nathan just flew me home this morning in a stealth bomber." Jess looked at Nathan, his disgust barely disguised. "What seems to be the problem?"

"Can't you see? I'm on the verge of double pneumonia, and all these numbskull doctors are good for is telling me they can't help because I'm allergic to every medicine known to humankind."

"I see. Well, I think we can do something about that." Jess reached out and touched the president's forehead. "Hmmm, little fever there. Well, you'll be back to normal quickly, sir. I guarantee it."

"I'd better be. For what we've paid you, I never should have gotten this sick to begin with."

"Trust me, sir, I'll never go on safari again, and you'll be your old self in a few hours. You might try to get some sleep."

At nine o'clock the next morning there was an emergency meeting of the cabinet and the most senior top-level officials. Nathan had been summoned a little before eight. The president was standing stark naked on a chair in front of an open office window facing Pennsylvania Avenue. The cool April breeze floated the curtains in long tails. A small crowd stood on the sidewalk outside the iron fence, pointing and exclaiming. A news van with a satellite setup on the roof screeched to a halt, and three people jumped out and started setting up cameras.

How the man had managed to get the window

open was a mystery to all. The windows in the White House were bulletproof glass and sealed shut.

"Birdie. See birdie, Mama? Ooooohhh."

The president of the world's greatest superpower was spouting gibberish, and whenever his wife or the doctor or one of the Marine guards tried to haul him down, he screamed obscenities and swatted at them with a length of two-by-four that had come from heaven knows where. His mind was apparently gone.

So was Jess.

Before the driver had closed the van's door, Jess slipped the tongue of his sneaker into the latch. He'd cut it off using the serrated edge of the paper towel dispenser in the john. The boy waited until he was certain they'd cleared the city; then, at the first stoplight, he quickly opened the unlatched door he'd been holding shut, ran around to the driver's door, and opened it before the man could react. The young giant grabbed the man by the neck and willed him unconscious. Spock couldn't have done it better. The man would wake up the next day in the back of the van, which would be parked at a shopping center.

Jess recognized the village of Ada. He was in the foothills of the mountains and not far from his own home. It took him about fifteen minutes, and as he turned up the long drive, the clock on the dash said it was ten-thirty.

"Mom—Dad!"

He knew that he only had an hour or so before

the alarm went out. With hugs and kisses, he explained what had happened over the last few months, ending with the fact that he had temporarily driven the president of the United States insane.

"He'll be okay in a couple of weeks. It's going to be interesting what they do about him in the meantime though."

Stephanie was the first to speak. "Jess, how could you? It's going to make a fugitive out of you, maybe for the rest of your life."

"Steph, I told you he'd get even. Jess, you should have left him that way a lot longer than a couple of weeks. The man's a buffoon. Neither your mom nor I voted for him."

"Mom, don't worry about it. Nathan needs me desperately. I'm like an addiction to him. I'll stay on the run until I feel like smoothing things over with him. By then, I'll have figured out how to make him do things my way, if at all. Maybe I'll suddenly lose my power or something." He grinned at them, seemingly unworried that he had just driven the president of the United States insane and the government into a panic that would have to be hidden from the world press.

Much of the depression had dissipated, and Jess's eternal optimism overcame some of his mother's apprehension. Shaking her head, she finally smiled at him and said, "Well, I never said we were a normal family—starting the day you healed Choctaw. What are we going to do now, Kiddo?"

"I'm going to take a long vacation and see this country and maybe a few others. I've got plenty of money. All I've got to do is keep out of their way. That shouldn't be too hard. We can meet from time to time. I'm sure I can sneak home. It won't be forever."

But it wasn't going to be that easy.

# 9

"Send me Chen!"

The fifty-five-room mansion sat on three hundred acres overlooking the Delaware River. Built in 1807 by Patrick Lanahan, a merchant who had made a fortune exporting and importing jewels, perfumes, and spices to a nation struggling hard to spend its newfound wealth, the home originally contained nineteen rooms, not including three indoor privies. The War of 1812 saw enormous profits and the addition of twenty more rooms and one hundred acres on either side of the original seventy-five. By the time the Civil War was in full swing, the mansion belonged to an arms merchant who owned a chain of gunpowder factories. In 1911, the arms merchant died from consumption, and the estate was sold to Francis Calhoun, the great-grandfather of its present owner.

Calhoun had built a chain of banks across the Northeast, a chain of meat-processing plants across the Midwest, and a chain of furniture factories across the South that used the wood from his own forest plantations. Over the years, the Calhoun family had added more rooms and land. Francis Calhoun, IV, was the last of the line. His bed had been moved to the large exercise room in the west wing to accommodate tons of the finest medical equipment money can buy. In spite of a platoon of doctors and nurses, the crusty old millionaire was slowly fading.

"Get me the Chinaman—now!"

"We've called him, sir. I'm sure it will be soon."

A rare form of cancer had spread from his prostate to his liver to his bones. Because Calhoun had had an aversion to doctors since childhood, the disease had gone undetected until too late for chemotherapy and radiation treatments. Over the course of three years he spent in excess of $1.5 million on quack cures and miracle home remedies. The legitimate health care and equipment had cost considerably more than that.

Dr. Andrew Manney, Ph.D., read about the terminally ill millionaire in Forbes. Manney had replaced Dr. Hoehn Rabin, the medical statistician on Dr. Fielder's research staff, after Rabin was killed in a freak auto/train wreck at a remote country crossing. Even though Manney had been working for several years for the National Health Organization and held a crypto clearance, Nathan had the man screened closely by the FBI. Unfortunately, bookies do not keep records accessible to the FBI, and because Manney was crafty enough to hide his compulsive gambling habit from the public-at-large, the bureau boys never found out about it. Hired to compile the tons of information already assimilated on the miracle healer in order to justify the amount of money already spent by Nathan and the president, Manney started work a little over a month after Jess had quit.

"Andy, they're foreclosing on the house."

"What?"

His wife of nineteen years was waiting for him in the foyer of their Washington suburb home. She was surrounded by suitcases. She continued in her half-scream, half-whine, "I can't take it any more. You've gone through everything we've got. There's not even enough money to buy the kids school clothes. I've had so many checks bounce, I've lost track. You need help and you won't get it. The boys and I are going to my sister's. I'm filing for divorce. I'm going to make sure they garnish your paycheck so you can't throw it all away. At least we'll have something."

"Dorothy, I'll get the money if you'll just give me a little time."

"Yeah, the same way you've been trying to get out of debt for the last two years. It won't work, Andy. Gambling's a losing proposition."

The statistician's addiction had got worse and worse until by the time he started his new job with a pay increase of twenty percent, he was in debt over

$200,000 just to the bookies. In spite of the Official Secrets Act he had signed, and the possibility of a long prison sentence, he contacted Calhoun's personal physician and suggested a meeting, alluding to a secret government testing program that guaranteed spectacular results. The doctor was skeptical but not as skeptical as Manney was convincing. With a little discreet checking the physician found out there was, indeed, a secret laboratory in the basement of one of the wings of Walter Reed Medical, and the old man went for it. "You actually work with this miracle boy?"

"I work with his records, sir. I've never personally met him."

"What does he do?"

"He heals—anything, everything. You've got to see it to believe it. Animals, plants, and people."

"Terminally ill? I've had my hopes smashed enough. If you're lying—setting up a con, you'll never work again for the government or anyone else. I've got a little clout left."

"I can only report what I see in my job every day, Mr. Calhoun. Do you remember two months ago—the little woman who had been in the iron lung for fifteen years because of polio?"

"Yes. It was all over the news. She got her college education in spite of it—wrote a book or something."

"I'll give you the number of her personal physician. She's in perfect health and is holding down a full-time job as a paralegal. They relocated her to Denver. The NSA made sure her miraculous cure never made the papers. They're protecting their own interests."

"Interests? Since when have the federal bureaucrats had any interest in anything except fleecing the American public?"

"Exactly. If the kid becomes public property, they couldn't keep him for their exclusive use any more."

"What are you talking about?"

"I mean they use him to heal the president and top-level officials whenever they get a cold or tennis elbow. I have all the records, including the boy's very thick personal file, his history, behaviors, psychological profiles, addresses of his relatives and friends, and every single healing he's performed since he started working for them over a year ago. I will sell you the information on him. After that, it's up to you."

The deal was struck, and Manney received an advance. He would duplicate the necessary records over the next few days, smuggle them out of the lab, and deliver them to the millionaire personally. If Calhoun and his staff were convinced, the statistician would become a wealthy man.

"He won't do it for money, sir. That much I know. He's already a millionaire, and he's only nineteen."

"He'll do it, one way or another. Get me Chen!"

Brian Chen was the product of a Vietnamese army

lieutenant and an American nurse. They met at an American embassy cocktail party at the height of the war. Amanda Tandy, twenty-two and cursed with a face that would stop an eight-day clock, couldn't be choosy. Four tequila sunrises and she was game for anything. She considered an abortion seriously but was never quite able to bring herself to do it. Because she was thin, she had been able to hide the pregnancy for six unbelievable months—wearing baggy uniforms, showering alone, and undressing in the dark. She was just beginning the third trimester when a mortar round landed twenty feet from the tent where she was working. She took seven pieces of shrapnel in the legs, was operated on, and was sent home. Her secret revealed, she was released from the army with a medical discharge. One month later she gave birth to a premature baby. Wanting nothing to do with the child, she gave the baby his father's last name and signed papers at the Sisters of Mercy Diocese in Baltimore, and the child's hospital bills became the basis for a lawsuit between the U.S. government and the Catholic church. The boy spent the next eighteen years in orphanages. Had he not been biracial, he probably would have been adopted.

"Mr. Chen, Francis Calhoun's attorney has been trying to get you all morning. He is bonkers-frantic." The secretary took a large wad of bubble gum out of her mouth, dropped it into the wastebasket, and immediately untwisted the waxed paper ends of another piece.

"Yeah. The batteries are shot again in the cellular. I wasn't able to get to a pay phone. What's he want?"

"Here's the number."

At age eighteen, and large for his age, Brian Chen enlisted in the Marines. He attended night classes wherever he was stationed and finally received a degree in forensic psychology. At age twenty-one, he was given his discharge and used veterans' benefits to pay for his graduate degrees. Bitter at being turned down for countless jobs because of his color, or lack of it, he found out that the FBI was under an order to hire more minorities. For the next ten years, he learned all the tricks of learning everything there was to know about anyone—congressmen, conglomerate owners, or conga players. He learned how to maintain surveillance without the subject's knowledge and how to find people who did not want to be found—mobsters, spies, embezzlers, and bank robbers. When he finally realized the white boys weren't ever going to let him do anything more than retrieve and survey, he resigned. He applied for a private investigator's license, and using money squirreled away over the years, he opened his own office in downtown Baltimore. Because he was intelligent, resourceful, and brilliantly sneaky, inside six months he tripled his FBI salary doing the same things he'd done for the government. Millionaire Francis Calhoun had used the Asian-American's talent on several occasions.

"Chen."

"Yes."

"Mr. Calhoun would like to see you."

"When would be convenient."

"Five minutes ago—hurry!"

Chen was in his Jaguar and on his way to the millionaire's mansion inside five minutes. He knew that the old man didn't have long to live.

By the next morning he reported that the boy had escaped from the NSA and that the government was about to crank up a full-scale search.

Two days later, Andrew Manney delivered a file that detailed everything there was to know about Jess Waterson. Someone had carefully detailed how the young giant quit the government because of Lottie's miscarriage and that Jess was probably still very much in love with her—why else would he resign and go off on a tangent? The file also included a great deal of recently dated material about Lottie Beringer. Evidently the NSA thought Jess might try to contact her.

"I want him before they get their hands on him! I want him brought here. Unlimited resources, Mr. Chen. You understand? I don't care if it costs millions. Write your own check if you find him. I want him fast!"

Chen began the usual credit card checks to see if he could pick up a trail. There was none. He tapped into the telephone of Jess's parents. The NSA quickly discovered the tap, and although they didn't know where it came from, they wanted exclusive rights.

They disconnected it. Chen wasn't disturbed. If the boy was going to be found through a telephone conversation with his folks, with access to unlimited manpower and resources, the NSA would beat him to the kid hands down. Besides, while reading Jess's file, Chen quickly came to the conclusion that this kid was not a normal nineteen-year-old. With unlimited funds, Chen hired a small army of agents to stake out dozens of places where Jess might turn up, including the cottage in the Adirondacks that belonged to Lottie's family. Chances were slim that they'd find him this way, but at least they'd know where he wasn't. Finding him was only half the problem. Once they had him, the kid would have to be tricked into using his powers. According to Manney's files, force would be a waste of time. Chen began turning over idea after idea on how to set the snare. All the plans centered around his secret lure, and if they could just glimpse the kid long enough to dangle the bait, Jess wouldn't stand a chance.

# 10

Unfortunately, the detective's plans went into a holding pattern. You can't hit what you can't see.

Jess drove the Cherokee north all night. The next morning he bought a tarp for it and left the Jeep covered in the far corner of a garage in downtown Ottawa. He then took a taxi to within a few blocks of a small printing shop on a back street in Hull. The rest of the way, he walked. His destination didn't need to appear on the taxi's log. Using a pay phone, his father had already called ahead to an old friend from naval intelligence days, and the forger was in the process of creating Jess a passport and Canadian driver's license along with a Canadian birth certificate, baptismal certificate, and social security card. The address on the license was real. If, by chance, the authorities checked out the address, someone would verify that Jess lived there. Because the forger used texture-correct papers, the documents would pass all but the most scrutinizing inspections, and these could only be done in a high-tech lab. When Jess offered the man the going rate, he was turned down.

"Consider it a favor to your father, young man. He did me a turn or two over the years."

Jess boarded a nonstop flight to Paris. In Paris he obtained his temporary European driver's license and bought a top-of-the-line BMW motorcycle. After asking enough questions, he found one of the few barber shops in Paris that would dye his hair in red, blue, and green stripes, then style it in a "chicken." On a last-minute whim, he had his eyebrows dyed black. Paris' version of the Yellow Pages led him to a theater supply company where he bought a medium-length coal-black beard to wear until his own could grow long enough, at which time he'd have to dye it black. He also bought two small silicone pads to fatten his cheeks along with the latex compound and makeup necessary to change the width of his nose and add beetling above the eyebrows. Experimenting each day with the makeup, he found a combination that rendered him so unlike himself he could have effortlessly fooled his own mother.

Constantly pricked by homesickness, Jess called home daily to tell his folks he was safe and to assure them that he would continue to call over the next few weeks while he was "enjoying" his "vacation." Uncle Sam still lacked the wizardry to trace overseas phone calls with any speed. With direct dialing, all that could be determined was that the call had originated somewhere across the pond.

From France, he pointed the motorcycle south and spent ten weeks sightseeing as spring completed its glorious work and summer mounted its campaign to tear it all down. Wherever he went, he drew attention, but in drawing such vivid attention to himself he was actually deflecting any chance of the NSA recognizing him.

"Big guy. Punker, biker. You shoulda seen the hair. No, no way. Who'd you say you was lookin' for? Naw. Not even close. Big though." It was exactly the kind of disguise that would make it impossible for the NSA to believe that underneath lay their peripatetic experiment. They would be convinced that the last thing he'd want would be to draw attention to himself, wherever he was.

Jess skipped some countries because he had no interest. Others, like Turkey, he skipped because of the bribes that would be necessary just to travel normally like any tourist who was driving an expensive motorcycle. It wasn't worth the hassle. Besides, he'd already had enough of the region's heat in Greece. Even in early summer the Mediterranean heat can be worse than Number One Barbecue in the lower bowels of Hades.

He turned back north, and skirting the problems in what used to be Yugoslavia, he zigzagged through the former Eastern Bloc into Austria to cross into Germany just north of Salzburg. Wary of the efficiency of Nathan's contacts in England, he decided not to tempt fate in the British Isles. Perhaps some other time. On the first of June he found himself a few miles from Hamburg, near a small town called Gutmesser where he ran into the Steisser family—literally.

Jess was paralleling the Elbe, enjoying the scenery immensely. Most of the river valley was flat, although from time to time there were hills lining the banks. An endless line of ships, tugs, and barges steamed in both directions. He stayed away from the main routes as much as possible. In Germany even remote country roads were well maintained.

The road led away from the river for several miles, and the countryside became flat and uninteresting. Jess spotted a wooded lane that had to lead toward the water, and he slowed and turned into it. Standing among the hardwood trees on either side of the path were large patches of wild rhododendron. June swirled them at the boy's senses in a crazy kaleidoscope of colors ranging from yellows to purples.

Inhaling spring's special perfumes, compacted and concentrated by forty miles an hour, Jess was climbing a small hill with only a fraction of his attention. The river tantalizingly reappeared briefly through a break in the woods, so he knew he was traveling in the right direction. Eager to see the water again, he was also driving a little faster than safety required. But then what nineteen-year-old doesn't have fast enough reflexes to get out of virtually any situation life affords? As the bike broke over the top of the hill, without warning Jess found himself plowing straight into the middle of a large, closely packed flock of sheep. Animals scattered in every direction, and several of them were not using legs. Stunned with surprise, he veered to the right and hit the front brake. The bike's back end reared into the air, and the boy flew over the handlebars and went suborbital. With the whole world to land on, Murphy's Law threw the giant at the only human within half a mile—the shepherd! The old man tried to dive out of the way, but the two-hundred-sixty-pound missile landed in a cross body block on spindly old legs. There was a sharp double-crack—the sound of large, dry twigs being snapped over a knee in preparation for a bonfire.

*"Edsel! Dummkopf!"* Two dogs barked wildly to reinforce the string of expletives that followed.

*"Absteigen Sie mich!"*

As the merely scraped-up boy struggled to shaky feet, a great deal of pain was only too evident in the shepherd's eyes.

*"Es tut mir Leid! Es tut mir Leid!"* Jess's German was limited, but he knew how to say, "I'm sorry," and he'd heard *Dummkopf* in old war movies. He never thought anyone would actually say it. Jess quickly reached for the useless legs to run his hands up and down both of them. The old man screamed in pain. There was a futile give and floppiness that confirmed the sharp cracks.

*"Schmerz?"* Understatement.

*"Glaube es, Dummkopf!"*

There it was again. The old man was calling him an idiot. Fair enough. He was an idiot!

"Do you speak English?"

"Yes. You fool, go call *den Krankenwagen*—the ambulance! You have broken both my legs!"

"Mister, I am truly sorry. I . . ."

*"Und meine Schafe! Oh nooooo!"*

Jess couldn't see any that were dead, but several were on their sides struggling to get up to no avail. The dogs were barking wildly and circling the scattered flock to get it back together. One of them ran to an injured lamb and began whimpering softly as he tried to nuzzle it back to its feet.

"I will fix this! I will fix this right now!" Jess was on the verge of tears himself.

Managing to sit, the old man began wailing and waving his hands at the sheep as if to gather them in his arms.

*"Meine Schafe!"* His own injuries seemed to be secondary to him. If Jess had not been experiencing serious panic and an overpowering anguish over the pain his carelessness had produced, he would have put the man and his sheep on the slow-heal timetable and made an exit. However, he had caused this problem, and it was up to him to fix it as quickly as possible. All his life he had allieviated pain. He had never been responsible for hurting someone else this seriously.

With his hands still on the old man's legs, the young healer quickly repaired the broken bones and accompanying trauma. He also fixed several other major and minor problems that had plagued the poor farmer for years—rheumatoid arthritis; total deafness in one ear, partial in the other—the result of a British howitzer shell in World War II; a bad pyloric hernia; colitis—his large intestine had been operated on twice for adhesions; heart disease—the farmer had been doctored for high blood pressure for forty years, and both sides of the heart had been damaged by heart attacks. Rarely could he walk up a flight of steps or even get out of a chair without becoming severely fatigued. To top it off the shepherd was missing two fingers. One of his own men had shot them off by mistake the day before his unit surrendered at Darmstadt.

Jess also triggered the proper genes to command the muscle, bone, blood and nerve tissue to regenerate new fingers. It would take three months, but the farmer would be astounded, as would everyone in his family and the *Bierhaus* in the nearby village, at the fact that he was growing two new fingers—unheard of in the annals of medicine!

The boy left the shepherd sitting in the road and went quickly to the injured sheep. There was little sense in holding back now. Why did he have to panic and heal the old man all at once? Dumbhead was putting it mildly! Jess placed his hands on the animals one by one and healed their injuries. The motorcycle had not only struck several, but it had also slid into the flock and broken and sprained a number of legs. By the time the boy reached the last two sheep, the farmer was standing beside him, exclaiming excitedly in German.

"*Wer sind Sie?*" The old man was shaking a pointed finger and glowering at the young giant with the Italian-flag haircut standing straight up.

"Excuse me?"

"Who are you?"

"My name is Jess. I am deeply sorry for the pain I've caused you and your sheep. I was careless." He ran his hands over the body of the last injured animal.

"Who are you?"

"Just a man." Jess stood up and asked, "What is your name?" He smiled and stuck out his hand. He wasn't too certain what the old man was going to do.

The farmer hesitated, then broke into a smile himself. He felt incredible! This boy had done something miraculous, and it went far beyond just repairing two legs that he knew, beyond a shadow of a doubt, had been badly broken. There were no more exotic combinations of pain swirling around his body—and the fatigue was gone! So was the shortness of breath. He took Jess's hand, pumped it, let go, and began to run and shout, "*Stiesser. Ich bin Wilhelm Stiesser.*" He danced and jumped. Then he began skipping around in a circle, singing, hollering.

"*Ich bin geheilt! Frei!* I am healed! All the pain is gone!"

The healed sheep returned to the flock, which the dogs had herded down the road toward the gate to the pasture. Jess watched the old man with amusement. He was not a little fearful at what was going to happen next. He would have to do some serious riding in order to put as much distance between him and this man as possible. If the miraculous cures hit the news media, there'd be no peace.

The farmer finally ran out of steam and returned to the boy. The old man's face gleamed with excitement.

"You must come home with me! You must meet Marthe! Please come and eat supper with us. Please come!"

"*Herr* Stiesser, I'd be delighted."

At least he would have the opportunity to try to talk the German out of going public with what had happened. Who knows?

The next morning Jess left the small farmhouse with a sack full of sausage, cheese, homemade pumpernickel bread, apple pie, and a plastic jar of apple cider. Jess had worked his miracle on the farmer's wife. She had been in almost as bad shape as the old man. Severe emphysema— caused by working in the coal mines as a young girl—kept her in bed much of the time. Also, unknown to her, there had been an advanced malignancy in her right breast.

Jess knew he had no right to ask them to keep the

miracles a secret. He did ask for a couple of days' head start.

On June 7, Jess entered Russia by way of Finland. He'd spent three days driving through Norway, then four in Sweden. Sweden appeared to have been scoured squeaky clean. There was no poverty in the socialist country, and all medical care was free. Why not, when sixty percent of personal incomes went for taxes. The huge, all-night ferry had taken him and the bike across the Gulf of Bothnia to Finland.

Because the Russians were eager for tourist money, they'd finally computerized the visa applications. Russia was one of the few countries that still required a visa. The European Community had all but eliminated borders in the remainder of Europe. Also the currency had been standardized.

As soon as he crossed the Russian border, Jess wished he'd left Mother Russia off the list of things to see. Any roads that weren't main thoroughfares were potholed and in poor condition. Also, it wasn't easy to find restaurants, especially ones that didn't give him a two-day stomachache. He drove from St. Petersburg to Warsaw in two and a half days. By the time he reached Poland, he had given up eating anything but fruit. The few gas stations had rest rooms that belonged in a cesspool. He was carrying a roll of paper towels from home in order to clean up from the diarrhea that assaulted him in the pine forests lining the road.

Not a day went by that he didn't have to work hard at pushing Lottie out of his mind. He carried on countless imaginary conversations that would get well into swing before he'd realize it, balk, and push them out of his head. The dialogues covered everything from French cooking to Greek yachts to the pines of Finland. It was as if she were with him. After all this time, his feelings, if anything, had increased. It also seemed that the aching increased in direct proportion to how far away from her he was. He finally gave up and had the BMW crated and shipped to Vancouver. The following day he boarded a plane for Bombay. By the time he'd seen Singapore, Hong Kong, and Tokyo, he'd completely lost interest in traveling. He booked a seat for Vancouver. He looked forward to the normalcy and predictability of North America. In the three months he'd been traveling, he'd never once worried about Nathan finding him. It's a great deal more difficult than the way it's done on television and in the movies.

It had been a very tough three months for Brian Chen. He'd drawn nothing but blanks. Without the phone tap on the boy's parents, the private investigator was flying on instruments. He discarded plan after plan to sucker Jess in. He had to have some kind of contact with the boy. Calhoun was all over his case.

"Mr. Calhoun, I've got over a hundred men on the payroll. They're watching every acquaintance the boy has ever made. I've got a dozen phones tapped, including his former girlfriend's. The Lear is standing on twenty-four-hour alert."

"Not good enough! Get more men. Throw around some money. I'm dying, Mr. Chen. I don't have years or months. I've got weeks if I'm lucky!"

"We know he's either overseas or using a phone where we can't trace the calls. I had Manney bug Dr. Fielder's phone. So far the tap has remained undiscovered. The NSA doesn't have a clue where he is either."

"Those apes couldn't find their way out of a one-holed outhouse! I want him found and I don't want excuses! Get some results, Chen, or you'll find yourself in a new line of work!"

The next day the detective finally got a break. The tap on Fielder's phone revealed that Jess had bought a satphone. The new high-powered version of a cellular phone worked off a series of satellites in orbit over the North American continent. Europe was in the process of launching its own system, but it would be another year before it would be operational. Confident that his calls could not be traced, the boy called the doctor just to make conversation. After several minutes of catching up, the doctor took a chance and told Jess that Lottie's grandmother had passed away at her cottage near Blue Mountain Lake. Jess said nothing, and there were several seconds of silence. Carefully noting the reaction, the doctor quickly changed the subject. Obviously, Jess had made little progress in coping with the loss of Lottie. The boy didn't know the grandmother well enough to be that bereaved. Jess finally said he needed to go.

"Jess, it's great to hear you. We miss you around here. You kind of took the heart out of things."

"Doc, you've got enough information to keep you busy for years. You don't need me. The only reason Nathan set the whole thing up was to use me for his own purposes. That was wrong!"

"I know, Jess, but don't be too hard on him. He does have the country's interests in mind even if he is out to feather his own nest."

"It's a big nest, Doc."

"Why don't you give him a call, touch base with him anyway? You know he can't trace the call, and from what I've heard, they've turned down the heat on you a little."

"Maybe. I'll have to think about it." Jess hated the things Nathan had done to him, but had long ago forgiven the little man. It might be good to hear the gravelly voice with its thick Brooklyn accent again. In spite of everything, Nathan was a likable man.

The doctor gave the boy the NSA agent's personal numbers.

Chen would have given a month's pay to hear that conversation. The head of the president's own security agency would probably have to change his underwear afterward.

It was the mention of the grandmother's Adirondack cottage along with the fact that Jess's phone had a caller ID feature that formed the basis of the plan that was developing in Chen's devious mind.

Once he got a couple of simple electronic devices, perhaps the detective could finally cast the bait. He was anxious to go to work.

The mention of Lottie's grandmother and the Adirondack cottage had triggered another wave of hurt in the young giant. He couldn't get her out of his mind no matter how hard he pushed. The images of the flat tire, the cottage, the wonderfully warm old woman, waterskiing, the cold lake water, and every other minute spent with Lottie hammered at his head relentlessly.

"Maybe I ought to go see her. Maybe talking to her would show me her flaws, and this ridiculous pounding would stop."

Midnight, five nights later, after driving across Canada to Detroit, then turning south for another day and a half, he was standing in front of Lottie's sorority house near University Park. He had carefully scoured the area for Nathan's cronies and was sure that there were none. Uncle Sam just didn't have the resources to be everywhere. Jess had noticed the scrofulous van with no front fenders parked the next block down the street, but it was in such bad shape that it had to belong to a college student. The government would never use something that gross.

Fortunately, both of Chen's agents were sound asleep. Chen had quantity enough, but the quality of his help left something to be desired.

The young giant paced up and down in front of the house, crossed the street and paced, sat on several park benches, then got up and paced beneath several trees in sight of the house. But there was not a deep enough well within him to confront the girl he was still deeply in love with, in spite of the fact that he hadn't laid eyes on her in eight months, eighteen days, and twenty-two hours. At one in the morning her light went out. At three he finally gave in to the depression, got on the motorcycle, and headed extremely cautiously toward home. By 4:30 A.M., he had covered the motorcycle with brush in a large patch of woods. He sneaked and crawled along hedgerows and fences for over a mile, and dawn was well in swing when he finally reached the backyard of the log cabin where he'd grown up. Two days later, he had almost caught his folks up on what he'd been doing for the last few months. However, when his mother brought up the topic of Lottie—had he seen her? Had he allowed the girl to explain? Had he . . . ?

"Mother, I don't want to talk about her!"

"Jess, you've got a problem here. Can't you see that?"

"Obviously."

"No! We're talking about two different things. You're talking about not being able to get over her.

I could tell that when you walked in the door. I'm talking about letting Lottie explain a few things to you."

"Never in all the lower bowels of basement hell! She blew it when she went to bed with another man! If I can live my life without sex until I'm married, then there's no reason she couldn't have! I'll find someone who has!"

"Jess, she did not . . ."

"Mother!"

"Jess, that baby was . . ."

"MOTHER!"

"You listen to me, young man. It's time you knew the truth and gave that girl a chance!"

"I won't listen, and she's had her chance!"

He had grabbed his jacket and barreled out the back door in broad daylight.

"Jess she was . . ."

"No!"

". . . raped!"

He was running across the field behind the house, hands over his ears. Within five minutes he was on the motorcycle and doing seventy miles an hour on a dirt road less than a mile from the house. He was so upset he didn't even notice the dark sedan with blackwalls parked on a hill that overlooked his log house. By sheer luck the sedan's occupant had been distracted by a phone call for the ninety seconds it took the boy to burst out the back door and run across the field in plain view.

Back in the log home a frustrated Stephanie Waterson was pacing and ranting to her husband.

"Jeff, I cannot believe that boy's thick head can house such unbelievable brilliance and pigheadedness at the same time! He can be so logical and normal Why won't he let us tell him the truth about that poor girl?"

Jeff had been in the study when the fireworks had started. He only made it to the kitchen in time to see Stephanie standing in the door hollering at her son.

"Steph, I don't know. I guess his analytical balance is trying to even out between miracle abilities and handicaps. This fanaticism is Jess's cross to bear. He's totally committed to remaining pure. He evidently cannot fathom the woman he loves not being that way too. If he only would let us—or her—tell him that she really has been. She's as amazingly unusual as he is. He won't find that again in this lifetime."

"Why won't he just let us tell him that?"

"He thinks you're going to say something else that will hurt him even more."

Jess once again lowered the thick iron shield over his head to block out all thinking except what was necessary to survive. He didn't remove it until he saw the sign that said, "Welcome to Canada." As his head cleared and his mind returned, he realized what a stupid stunt he'd just managed to get away with.

"Lucky. Very lucky. I might as well get a motel for the night, then go check on the Jeep in the morning. I'm only a couple of hours from Ottawa."

The next morning, after checking for surveillance for over an hour, the young giant finally convinced himself that they had not found the car. It was right where he'd left it, the tarp undisturbed beneath a thick layer of dust. The custom-made mountain bike had been in the back of the Cherokee for as long as Jess had owned the car, and it gave him an idea. He decided to find a self-storage garage to hide both the motorcycle and the Jeep, and after looking in the Yellow Pages he found what he was looking for only a few blocks away. He paid for a year's lease and was careful not to let the manager see him drive the vehicles inside.

The bike was in perfect condition as were all the supplies. He lubricated the chain and derailleurs with a Teflon-based lubricant, locked the garage door, and after looking briefly at a map he'd taken from the Jeep, he headed due east—toward Montreal. He would first see the eastern part of Quebec on the mountain bike, then perhaps enter the U.S. in Maine and tour the mountains of New Hampshire and Vermont. However, by the sixth day he began feeling a little vulnerable in the open. It was too flat. There were too many towns, too many people. If somebody did get onto him, he was helpless on the bicycle. With the motorcycle or the Jeep he might outrun them, but not on the bike. He'd long ago decided against using the rubber-mask disguise again. The latex itched, took a long time to put on, and was messy coming off. Hopefully, the black dye and blue contacts he had begun using when he arrived in Vancouver would be enough.

*Wrong!*

The scare in the french-canadian town with the canal confirmed that safety could only be found in the deep woods. Using night's protection, and believing nathan's cronies would think he'd panic and head immediately south toward new york state, Jess turned instead toward the southeast and sprinted the fifty-five miles to the vermont border. Avoiding the government entrance center at richford, he crossed a couple of miles to the west on a mountain trail just as the sun cleared the trees.

Once he reached the serious mountains, with their back roads and trails, he began to feel safe, safe enough to lose the contacts, wash the black rinse out of his hair, and shave his beard. He'd grown tired of looking like someone else. Anyway, the contacts hurt his eyes, and like the latex, the beard itched in the summer heat.

It wasn't long before the bike began to take on a mind of its own. He found himself helplessly heading west—toward New York and the Adirondacks—Blue Mountain Lake, for sure.

"Lottie, what in the world am I going to do?" A three-gallon sigh accompanied the question.

# 11

Four days after he had made a new woman out of Eva Bartlett on Tinker's Ferry Road, Jess was pedaling around the northern end of Lake Champlain. In spite of his not being able to avoid some main roads, going around the lake was safer than taking the ferry. If someone spotted him getting on the boat, he'd face a welcoming party at Port Kent on the New York side.

In Rouses Point he picked up the genesis of Route 11. The federal highway came within fifty miles of his home on its sixteen-hundred-mile plunge to New Orleans. As soon as possible—within a dozen miles—he turned south on a state road and headed toward the mountains. As they grew before him, he was able to forgo the blacktop for back roads and state-maintained trails. Six days later he was in the village of Long Lake to get supplies. "Lake Taxidermy" read the sign on the storefront next to the little market. There was a stuffed bobcat in the window. The memory of the rabid mountain lion practically taking his arm off a week and a half before was still vivid in the young giant's mind. The memory of Lottie and Blue Mountain Lake just a few miles down the road was even more vivid than the cougar.

Dave Longtree locked the front door of the post office for the day. He had turned thirty-five two days before, the same day his divorce was final. "Cruel and unusual punishment" the decree had read—on his part—in spite of the fact that she'd fooled around on him for years and had finally left with a pharmaceutical salesman from St. Louis. Cruel and unusual was the only way the state would grant a divorce. Dave wasn't sure whether Lilah's antics had anything to do with the premature white in the mutton chops that cascaded down either side of his face into the waterfall double chins. He stuffed the keys in his front pocket, unmindful, as usual, that he was still wearing his granny glasses halfway down a cherry nose with the earpieces perched precariously on the tops of his ears. If he'd had a beard, he could have passed for Santa Claus at the North Pole near Lake Placid. Dave had actually been offered the position about three months before.

"I'd never be able to keep from shooting all those deer come hunting season." Santa's Workshop had a number of reindeer wandering around looking for handouts from the tourists.

Dave walked up the street to the small market to

figure out what to get for supper. He'd quickly grown tired of racking his brains every night. One thing about Lilah, she sure could cook. Dave's forty-pound tire and its supporting accoutrements testi-fied to that. Supper needed to be something that would help him lose weight. Rabbit food was a fate worse than being forced to watch his poker partner Sonny Nealie gulp down three cheeseburgers, a dou-ble order of home fries, a bowl of rice pudding, and two pieces of apple pie—just for lunch! And the man never gained an ounce! At home there were plenty of trout in the freezer, along with half of last year's venison and some bearburgers, but he hadn't thawed anything out and didn't like what the microwave did to wild meat.

Dave spotted Jess in a heartbeat, and all thoughts of food went out the window. With $50,000 riding on the boy's capture, the postmaster had taken time to memorize the telephone number along with the three different poses on the flyer. The boy's physical measurements left no doubt about it. Dave was on the pay phone in the store's back corner before Jess even got to the counter with his purchases.

Ordinarily, Nathan's office would have to direct the state police or the sheriff's patrol to pick up Jess and hope that they didn't bungle the job. However, by the most incredible stroke of luck, the vice presi-dent was vacationing at a fishing lodge only five miles from Long Lake. There were scores of extra law enforcement officials in the area in addition to a dozen secret service agents.

When the call from the whispering man came into Nathan's office, it was screened and determined to be genuine, and the likable agent from Brooklyn was tracked down at a cocktail party for the Central American peace contingent at the Fairmont Hotel.

Within four minutes he reached the satphone of the secret service agent coordinating security with the local officials, and in no uncertain terms Nathan made it clear that if Jess escaped, the agent would spend the remainder of his career right there in the mountains. "This is a matter of the utmost national security, Trousdale. This boy is of more importance to the U.S. government than you can possibly imagine."

"Yes, sir. We'll get him. The VP is well secured for the night, and I can spare some men along with the locals."

Although he had not been allowed to observe, Trousdale had been on duty both times Jess had visited the president. The before and after were obvious, and after discarding several alternatives, the agent kept to himself what he believed the boy had most likely been doing with the president of the United States. It was illogical and nothing short of miraculous, but there it was—the Old Man had been sick as a dog one minute and gung-ho well the next! Trousdale had no doubt at all that Nathan would make good on his threats. The boy was a gold mine.

Only fifteen minutes after Dave made his call, three state police cars and a dark green sedan with black-walls came silently screaming down the long hill, across the silver bridge, and into the village at sixty-five miles an hour. Coincidentally, four reporters from the press corps covering the vice president's vacation were walking down the street from the old resort hotel to the restaurant next door to the market. They were in a perfect position to watch the cars come to a quick halt in front of the market.

Jess had taken his supplies to his bike, then, a minute later, came back into the store to ask if he could use the rest room. He was watching a fast runabout on the lake and not looking where he was going when he collided hard with Dave, who was running to the door to see just which way the young giant was heading. In spite of Dave's spare tire, he was still significantly outweighed. Glasses flying, he had bounced off the boy and gone down in a pile on the floor.

"Excuse me," he yelped. "Excuse me, sir! Excuse me!" He finally found his glasses.

"No, excuse me. I'm really sorry." Jess reached down to help him up. With the postmaster back on his feet and obviously none the worse for the wear, Jess asked the elderly lady behind the counter where the rest room was.

"It'th in the thtoreroom in the back. Go through that expenthive antique door behind the bread counter and thwing a hard right."

"Thanks."

"Wait! I ain't done."

Jess stopped in his tracks.

The old lady continued, looking at her fingernails in exaggerated nonchalance. "Then go down the hall to the gymnathium. Go through the gym and look for the third door on the right."

A grin started to form on the young giant's face as she continued. "Take that and go down the long hall to the fourth door on your left. That'th the boiler room. Onth you get in the boiler room ith eathy to get lotht, tho pay attention! Find the door at the back. That'th important! That'll lead you to an enormouth hall that we thometimeth uthe to keep the animalth warm on cold nighth. Then . . ."

"I get the picture! I give! I give!"

She finally looked up at him and grinned.

The young giant found the "antique" door. Its scars revealed at least three colors of paint. It scraped on the floor as he opened it, and Jess noticed that two of the three hinges were loose. He found himself in a storeroom. The john was over to the right in the corner.

Dave Longtree got more and more nervous. They'd better hurry. The boy was a walking $50,000 check signed by Uncle Sam himself, and Dave already had a new houseboat picked out.

"Dave, you gonna buy thomethin' or are you jith workin' up the nerve to athk me to fool around with you all weekend again?"

Seventy-two-year-old Frances Paterson had owned the market for forty-five years. She had outlasted two husbands who had run it with her. With only a high school boy for part-time help, she still restocked and maintained the place by herself. Wrinkled and never without a cigarette, she kept her teeth in a jar on a shelf below the cash register. She had taken them out sixteen years before and had never put them back in because they hurt. Without them there was always that slight problem with the letter *s*. From behind the register she could not help noticing the postmaster's unusual behavior. The man had been walking around the store half-heartedly pawing at things, his eyes glued to the storeroom door.

The postmaster blushed and said, "Yut, need some paprika."

"Paprika? We ain't got that kind of thtuff, you moron. Gwan down to IGA and leave me in peath."

Dave didn't have time for a comeback. The four cars pulled up at the front of the store, and he breathed a serious sigh of relief. He ran out the front door and in a stifled yell hollered, "He'th in the john! He'th in the john. Excuse me. He's in the john! He's in the back! Quick!"

Trousdale sent two of the state police officers to cover the back door, then with three of his own agents he barged through the store to the back room holding a hand up like a traffic cop to Frances, who was standing with her hollow mouth gaping like an open grave.

"Open the door, son! This is Agent Trousdale, United States Secret Service!"

No answer.

"If you don't open, we're going to break it down."

"Why don't you jutht try the knob, offither. It don't lock anyway."

The old lady had followed the men as far as the doorway.

Agent Trousdale did just that, and as the door swung open to reveal the ancient, foxed wallpaper of the small room, Dave Longtree almost had a heart attack. The room was empty.

The men quickly examined the storeroom, but there was nowhere to hide. There was a back door, though. They went through it and met the two state policemen outside.

"Didn't he come out?"

"Nope. Nobody."

"How long had he been in the john?" The agent was looking at Dave.

"Hadn't been in there three minutes before you pulled up. You got here fast."

"He obviously went out the back. Spread out! We find him or we all die a slow and agonizing death!"

The men left in several directions, one of them loping the few yards down to the public beach where a float with a diving board was anchored about sixty feet from shore. Two seaplanes were moored next

to private docks at one end of the beach. There were
no bicycle tracks in the sand. The shoreline behind
the half dozen stores and the restaurant quickly
turned to thick woods as the village main street made
a right-angle turn away from the lake to lead up a
steep hill in front of the high school. The other men
quickly covered the half dozen shops, the restaurant,
and the hotel to ask if a six-foot-ten-inch boy had
been seen. When they asked the four reporters if
they'd seen the boy, the reporters set up a barrage of
their own questions.

"Six-ten?"

"Who is he?"

"How old?"

"And the secret service wants him?"

"A kid?"

"Give us a break!"

"What in the world did he do, Trousdale?"

"Hey, wait up!"

The agents would not supply any information
beyond Jess's description. However, when the reporters discovered Dave Longtree, the postmaster
never had a chance. In a panic bordering on hysteria
at the possibility of losing so much money, he was
defenseless. No matter. It wasn't as if it were classified information. He gave them the circular with
Jess's pictures and descriptions along with the promise of the $50,000 reward for aiding in his capture.

The next day the wire services carried the head-
lines, "Uncle Sam Offers Big Reward for Kid.

Why?" The stories contained all the information on the flier plus a great deal of speculation. Nathan had to be sedated by the White House physician.

Had Jess not bumped into Dave Longtree, literally, the young giant might easily have ended up in Nathan's hideaway again. He had lost much of his sense of caution. He'd been all over Europe, around the world, across Canada, back home, back to Canada, Vermont—and there had only been the one-time possible problem a week before in the small town in Quebec. Actually, there was no proof that the man asking questions was more than a curious local. Jess had grown careless. The postmaster's overly solicitous reaction after the collision in the store's doorway triggered a latent alarm, and while the young giant was helping the man off the floor, he read the postmaster's mind. Trouble.

When Jess had entered the store's large back room, he knew time was short and that in the open it would only be a matter of time unless he could make the deep woods. That would be an iffy proposition. The six-by-six bathroom had been built into one corner of the storeroom, and the small room's ceiling was lowered more than seven feet below the storeroom ceiling. The bathroom walls carried upward to the storeroom's ceiling with some simple framing and a couple of leftover sheets of stamped tin. The material was one of the prevalent wall coverings in churches, offices, and stores in the late 1800s when the building had been constructed. Jess noticed one of the sheets was loose where it joined the outside wall. Perhaps the wood was dry-rotted, and tension from the tin sheet expanding and contracting with the temperature differences all those decades had gradually loosened the nails.

He quickly ran out the back door and up the narrow alley toward the store's front where the bike leaned against the alley wall. Unseen, he wheeled the bike back down the alley and in the back door. Standing on the ledge of a window that had been boarded up with plywood after the third burglary twenty years before, he was easily able to pry the tin away from the wood. There were only four nails in the sheet, and he removed them and stuck them in his pocket. With his tremendous strength he lifted the bike up and through the opening to set it on top of the rafters that carried the bathroom's ceiling. He then boosted himself up and through the opening to find a closed room the same dimensions as those of the bathroom below. There was enough space for the bike to rest catercorner and still leave room for Jess to stand on the rafters.

Now he needed some way to pull the tin sheeting back flush with the stud and pin it. He was about to dig a piece of gear cable out of the bike repair kit when he remembered the coiled length of stovepipe wire on the windowsill below. He lowered himself to the ledge, grabbed the wire, dusted off his footprints and any other sign of his presence, and quickly sprang up through the opening. Jess looped the two

ends of the six-foot piece of wire around the heads
of two nails, then threaded the nails through two of
their original holes in the tin. Even with the dry rot,
there was no way to make them go back into the
original holes in the wood without a hammer-rap on
the outside, so he bent the nails to the side to avoid
the holes. Pulling the wire allowed the sheet to snug
fairly well against the stud. Other than an inch of
thin wire running from two slightly tipped nail heads
to the edge of the tin and two innocuous empty
holes, there was no trace that the sheeting had ever
been loose. Because the whole operation was in a
dark corner and over eight feet from the floor, Jess
felt confident nobody would spot his handiwork. He
was wrapping the free end of the wire around an
exposed nail sticking out from the wall just as the
secret service agents burst into the room. Within two
minutes they were gone.

The old lady closed up shop at eight o'clock.
Padded with one of his packs, Jess had been able to
sit on the bike's crossbar and had not had to balance
on the rafters for an hour and a half. He could easily
hear the conversations from the customers and
everything Trousdale asked when he came back after
half an hour of searching to question the old lady.

"Mithith Franthith Leonie Paterthon," she told
the reporters. "One t in Paterthon. Paterthon'th
Market. Yur gonna put me on TV ain't cha? Make
thure you get a good thyot a the front of the thtore,
or I ain't giving you thquat!"

During the night, with his flashlight in his mouth, the young giant laid flooring in his hideaway using some dusty scraps of plywood that were leaning against a wall in another dark corner of the storeroom. He found a hammer and a large nail, and using a piece of rope from one of his packs he hung the bicycle from one of his walls. He drove the nail with only three well-spaced whacks. At three o'clock in the morning there was probably nobody to hear, but there was no sense in taking chances.

Mrs. Paterson opened the store at seven in the morning. By nine, with the running account of the exhaustive manhunt kept current by a steady stream of customers, Jess decided to make the small room over the john his home for a while. Mrs. Paterson did notice that the door to the storeroom now swung freely. The hinges had been tightened. She also noticed that the toilet didn't run anymore after flushing. For many years, she'd had to rattle the handle in order to make it stop.

The next morning she smelled varnish when she opened the front door. The door to the storeroom had obviously been sanded clean before it had been beautifully stained and varnished. It was gorgeous and looked like a real antique door. The supplies must have come from the old workbench in the storeroom. She also noticed that the last loaf of wheat bread on the bread shelf the night before was gone, along with a package of bologna, a box of cookies, and some batteries. A ten-dollar bill lay on the cash register.

"My, my. I love a mythtery. Let'th juth keep our mouth thyut, Franthith, and thee what happenth. That boy don't detherve whatever thoth goonth got in thtore for him anyhow."

Jess sneaked out for a midnight swim the next night. All day long the conversation had centered around helicopters, dogs, and the army reserve unit from Tupper Lake. He had watched through a small hole he'd drilled in the wall of his hideaway that gave him a direct look down into the store. All day long a steady stream of law officers traipsed in and out to buy soft drinks and snacks. There had also been a number of reporters, including a couple of television news teams. Francis Paterson talked about everything except her new tenant. Jess noticed that she lowered the bamboo window blinds that usually kept out the afternoon sun and left them down when she locked up.

The next morning, seven-eighths of the store's entire floor was freshly painted battleship gray. It hadn't had a coat in years. The lights in the dairy case and in the soft-drink case were working. The wiring had been fried in a lightning strike several months before. A note on the register said, "Need a quart of gray. Also three gallons for walls, your choice, along with drop cloths and a good brush."

Francis sent the high school boy to the hardware store for the supplies. The boy was half sick about it, just knowing he was going to have to do all that painting. Over the next three nights the floor was finished and the walls were painted along with the insides of the windows. With all that paint and the handsome stained door that led to the storeroom, the place began to take on a look of sophistication. It was a far cry from what it had been for as long as anyone could remember. "Out-of-town contractor. Cheap, too! Real cheap!"

Each night some food and more batteries were missing, and on the fifth night Frances decided to put a stop to that. Before she locked up, she left a turkey-sized roaster with a huge, still-steaming seven-pound beef roast and its accompanying juice-cooked vegetables on the counter next to the register. She had slow-cooked it all day in her oven at home. There was even a loaf of homemade bread and real butter. She also left Jess's ten-dollar bill on top of the roaster.

The next morning, the ten-foot antique counter that held the cash register and the quarter-round glass candy case was completely sanded.

"Need a quart of stain and half a gallon of varnish."

The following morning it was stained and varnished. The top of the counter, over three and a half feet wide, was one board cut from an eight-hundred-year-old oak in 1920. It looked spectacular.

A week went by. During the day, Jess read and slept in his hideout. Most important, he spent uninterrupted time in his seasons. It was wonderful—the communion, the heightening. At night he swam, walked the beach, called home on the satphone, and worked on Mrs. Paterson's store. He found some brass sheets in the storeroom and fashioned them into counter trim in several parts of the store. With all the visible varnish, the old-fashioned stamped tin walls, now painted dark red, the ceiling in light blue, and the windows and original gingerbread moldings and trim painted in kelly green, the room took on a nearly breathtaking turn-of-the-century look.

The law enforcement officials finally began to dwindle. They had searched the surrounding area in a thirty-mile radius, and much of it was deep woods. Nathan was unrelenting. He had pressure emanating straight from the White House.

The news media probed, speculated, and received nothing. After a week with nothing new, the story dropped off the back page.

Eleven days after Jess moved in, Long Lake was back to normal. The search had been called off. Nathan had accepted that the boy had somehow slipped through the iron blanket. As the old lady was busying herself to close, there was a soft, "Mrs. Paterson?"

"Jess!" His name had been national news for a week. Nobody knew why.

He thanked her for not turning him in and for the "lodging."

"I think I'll be okay as long as I travel after dark for a while."

"Young man, you have performed a real miracle around here. I long ago gave up on this place." Frances had started wearing her teeth two days before in anticipation of meeting her boarder.

"It does look great, doesn't it?"

"I haven't had so many compliments since I was eighteen. Come here and give old Frances a hug. Your mama know where you are?"

"Yes. I have a phone and I call my folks every night."

She reached for him, and he held her for the better part of half a minute. He could feel the collective infirmities of seventy years swirling inside her. There was the horrible pain of terminal lung cancer—the enormous difficulty in just breathing; there were heart disease, the usual arthritis; there were stomach problems, gall bladder, lower bowel—on and on the maladies roiled, and Jess knew every one by heart. A lot of her illnesses were the direct result of three packs a day. Frances Leonie Paterson had been hooked on cigarettes the day she was born, the legacy of a chain-smoking father and mother. With the pain she supported, most women would have given up long ago, opting for a nursing home or worse. All that difficulty and the old lady had kept her sense of humor.

It wasn't until the next afternoon that she realized she hadn't smoked a single cigarette in almost twenty-four hours. She began to feel better each passing hour. Forty-eight hours after the young giant said his good-byes, Frances noticed she was standing straight. There was no more pain in her limbs. And the ever-present nausea was gone.

"Odd."

The following day her breath returned. She awakened without the insidious pain in her chest. She hopped around the bedroom huffing and puffing in a serious attempt to provoke the stabs. No wheezing, no pain.

"Wo, Frantheth. What'th going on here?" The teeth had gone back in the jar.

By the fourth day, Frances Paterson was feeling like a teenager. She did the only logical thing and went to the doctor.

"Look here, Mrs. Paterson: This is your last X ray. See this dark area here . . . here . . . here?"

"Yut."

"Look at today's picture . . ."

"No dark."

"No kidding! You want to tell me how you managed that? You should have died in the not-too-distant future."

"Don't know."

That night before she went to sleep, Francis Paterson was sure she was, of all things, teething! Her gums hurt. She was sure she could feel teeth just under the skin. She wanted to chew on something.

"Bah. Can't be."

Jess had left the store at two in the morning. Blue Mountain Lake was only ten miles away, two hours of easy riding even in the mountains. With almost a full moon he didn't need the powerful halogen head lamp. The next morning the young giant was sitting under a large pine tree on the far side of the lake. The cottage was clearly visible. No one was there. Around noon he checked the caller ID on his sat-phone. Four numbers scrolled by—the numbers of people who had called. The fifth number almost gave him a heart attack.

# *12*

It was Lottie's number.

*She must have got the number from Mom.*

It all came back, sweeping over him in waves of unlabeled emotion that brought great tears. For once he was not going to let his pride and stubbornness stand in the way. He would call her.

"Hi, this is Lottie. I'm away from the phone right now. Please leave a message. Jess, if that's you, I must see you immediately. Please. Will you meet me at the place where we had lunch the first day we met? I'll be there on Tuesday, the thirteenth, at eleven. Please, please be there."

Jess couldn't believe his ears. He was at that very moment looking at the cottage where they'd had lunch the first day they'd met! And Tuesday was tomorrow! She must be on the way. What if Nathan was monitoring her answering machine? Jess had told Dr. Fielder about the first day with Lottie. Would the doctor remember? Would it be in Jess's file? Could Nathan find out? It would be taking a tremendous chance. Odd that Lottie would take that kind of chance. She would have known he was in the area from the news media and had waited until things died down. Still, she must be desperate. She didn't sound good. Her voice was shaky. Whatever the problem, he would fix it. He would forgive and fix. If she were still interested—she must be! What other reason could there be?

The week and a half he'd spent in the hideaway had brought him to the conclusion that he'd been selfish and wrong. He couldn't expect everyone to have the same standards that he did. They didn't have the same gifts that he had. She should at least be allowed to explain. What was it that Mom had kept trying to tell him?

Using the usual quarter can of insect repellent, he camped that night in the woods across the lake. The black flies had been unusually bad since he'd been in the mountains, but in spite of them and the mosquitoes, the first night out of his hideout he slept like a log. It had taken him all day to come down from the high and get over the excitement of hearing her voice. He'd carefully checked out the cottage to make sure no one was watching it. The bike had been left covered with the infrared-proof camo tarp and a pile of brush. Wearing his camo fatigues he'd silently moved around the lake to watch the area with binoculars. He'd changed positions several times to make sure he could see every possible hiding place. There were no government sedans, no camouflaged men in the woods, no periscopes in the lake. Jess was surprised that Nathan didn't have a permanent team staking it out. Perhaps the little man was finally losing interest or perhaps Uncle Sam just couldn't afford it any longer. The search for him in Long Lake must have cost a bundle, and Congress was probably getting very curious. After watching all day, he'd finally given up at dark and had gone back to his camp. After a light supper he'd gone to bed early.

He woke at 4 A.M. so excited he couldn't stand it. He mixed two dried breakfasts with water and heated them over the small Sterno stove. The sun hadn't even thought of coming up when he left the camp in pitch dark to follow the shoreline. He was determined to make sure the cottage wasn't under surveillance. He had to be absolutely sure that Nathan didn't have Lottie's phone bugged.

By 8 A.M. there was still no activity. The car wasn't there, so she hadn't come in late and stayed all night. She must have started very early in the morning to make the trip.

By ten o'clock, she still hadn't arrived. One thing was sure—there was no one watching the place. Jess had made absolutely sure of that.

Eleven. Try as he could he was unable to will the little red MG up the dirt road to the cottage.

Twelve. She must have had a flat tire. Heaven help! This would not be the time to have a wreck!

Two. Still no Lottie and Jess was beginning to

think she had got cold feet. No matter. He would wait. Love conquers all.

Five. What in the world was she trying to do to him? She could have hired a taxi and made it by now!

He called her number in Maryland.

"Hi, this is Lottie. I'm away from the phone right now, but if you'll leave your message, I'll get back to you. Thank you."

*What in the world is this woman doing to me? If something was wrong, unless she were unconscious or dead, she'd call me or she'd leave another message on the machine. Why her usual message?*

Seven. He called her home.

"Mrs. Beringer, this is Jess Waterson. How are you?"

With a heart beating in the upper one-seventies and a dry mouth, Jess explained that Lottie had left a message to meet him and that she hadn't shown up. Was she alright?

"She's fine, Jess. I just talked to her about an hour ago. She's at her sorority house studying for a test. Why don't you call her there?"

What in the world was going on! How could she do this to him? Obviously, she had got cold feet. She had made a fool of him and no way was he going to give her the satisfaction of crawling on his knees to ask her why.

The next morning he uncovered the bike and, after looking at the map, he headed for the deepest woods in the state of New York. There was nothing but wilderness cut only by a few trails and logging roads. Civilization and women who lied had yet to gain an entrance, and that was exactly how the young giant intended to keep things.

Three days later he did see a helicopter. It wasn't close and he was in more than enough cover to remain unseen, regardless of who it was. He'd taken his time and spent the entire three days on the forty-mile state trail that led around Little Moose Mountain. There weren't any moose in the area, but Jess saw numerous deer, a couple foxes, a few raccoons, a skunk, two porcupines, and countless squirrels and chipmunks. There had been only one backpacker on the trail. They'd briefly exchanged hellos as Jess rode by him.

The longer Jess rode, the angrier he became. What she'd done was not right. She'd never even had the decency to call him and explain. He'd checked the satphone every hour for three days looking for her number.

On the morning of the third day he'd ridden about a mile when he heard singing. From the distance it sounded either like a woman with a low voice or an Irish tenor. The trail led down the side of a mountain and into a small valley. It came within a few dozen yards of a lake. Through the trees Jess could see diamond-studded water scattering the summer sun. He left the trail, leaned the bike against a tree and slowly made his way through a stand of thick alders down to the lake's shoreline.

*"Had I only one wing of an angel, lopsided,
I'd fly straight to you."*

Facing the center of the lake, she was standing neck-deep in the water, washing her hair. Turning, she looped the shampoo bottle high in the air the twenty-five feet to the shore where it bounced in the sand and came to rest next to a pile of clothes and a pack. Then she ducked under the water probably to rinse off the soap. For thirty, then forty, then fifty seconds the woman didn't surface. The lake ironed itself free of ripples like a fastidious old maid smoothing a Sunday dress. At sixty seconds, Jess began to seriously entertain the thought of running and swimming to her rescue, but just as he was about to break cover, she surfaced fifteen yards from where she'd disappeared and began swimming toward the middle in a slow, efficient Australian crawl. After three minutes of this, she made a slow circle and swam lazily back. Touching bottom, she stood and walked out of the water—totally naked!

She was tall, very tall—six feet, maybe, and probably in her late twenties. Long, thick black hair matted around her neck and shoulders. Her body was lean, well-hardened, and perfectly proportioned, and her face, even without makeup, was that of a beautiful woman.

"You can come out now."

Jess was shocked. *How could she have possibly known he was there?* He was well hidden and totally embarrassed at being caught in the act of voyeurism. She seemed unconcerned about him and took her time drying off with the towel.

After a pregnant pause, he stood and stuttered, "Caught me. Sorry. I . . . a . . . didn't mean to . . . a spy, but you . . . "

"Forget it, Kid. There are only two models of Homo sapiens on Planet Earth. You're either model A or model B. If you're neither, or both, you've got a big problem. I never could understand all the secrecy when there are literally billions of both."

"When you put it that way, I guess it makes sense." He was barely able to maintain eye contact, and an entire hockey game was in full swing . . . He continued, "What are you doing way out here? How'd you get here? You're not supposed to see women like you in the deep woods." Thunderstruck, his voice was on the verge of pubescent cracking.

She dressed slowly, without embarrassment. Eyes smiling in warm amusement, she deflected his bigotry replying, "What are you doing out here? You're entirely too young to be away from your momma, too big to be crawling around in the brush and too blonde to be an abominable snowman."

Jess felt another stab in the sump, and he visibly

flinched. She continued, "Or, what's a nice little boy like you doing in a place . . ." She didn't finish the sentence. Her voice was husky and very low for a woman—in the range of some men. Sarcasm studded every word.

"Touché."

With her thick hair only partly dried, Jess could see she was, indeed, an extremely beautiful woman—on a par, and more, with many models he'd seen on magazine covers. Blue irises were surrounded by a black ring. Her nose had a slight hump to it. Coupled with the thick hair it gave her a feral, animal look—dominant, forceful. Perhaps she was a model. She had put on two tank tops, a tight blue one beneath a red one. Khaki walking shorts full of pockets reached half-way to her knees and she wore hiking boots with thick red socks. The long legs were well muscled and tanned.

"Well, where do we go from here, Kiddo? Now that you've seen me naked, we have to get married." Jess could feel the skin prickling on his face and knew he was blushing. This time she actually grinned at his embarassment.

With his dignity in the "Bargain Basement Bin," he made an attempt at salvaging the tatters and said, "My name's Jess."

"I know. Before I came up here, your mug was all over the tube. You're rather famous."

"Are you going to turn me in?"

She laughed. It was deep, throaty, genuine.

"I don't know. What's it worth to you?"

Jess let out a long sigh and said, "Enough to be a long ways away before anybody you can notify can get here."

"My name's Ursala. Ursala Tellum." She did not hold out her hand. "I've been alone on these trails for almost a week, and I wouldn't mind the pleasure of your company. If I promise not to send up coded smoke signals to summon Uncle Sam, will you tag along for a couple days?"

Jess was totally bewitched. Perhaps he deserved the company of this woman in view of what Lottie had just pulled. Anyway, he hadn't even talked to Lottie in over nine months, much less seen her. Maybe this would help him get her out of his system—once and for all. And maybe he was asking for serious trouble.

"You got a deal, but I hold all the matches. That way I'll know you're not starting a signal fire the first time my back's turned."

"Fair enough. Which way do you want to go? I don't have to be back to work until I feel like it."

"I don't know. Let's just follow our noses."

The next three days they spent hiking the trails together. Jess found a convenient place for the bike, hid it well, and took the supplies he needed with him. How could he possibly have known that a powerful transponder had been hidden beneath the bike's seat? It had been placed there the first night he'd camped across the lake from Lottie's cottage. Once he'd been lured to the area, finding the camouflaged bike and planting the transmitter had been easy. It had been accomplished by a full-blooded Mohawk Indian whose services Chen had used on several occasions. Jonathon Halfsnake McCarthy could sneak a herd of giraffes down the full length of a football field during the middle of the fourth quarter without them being seen.

Chen had paid a computer consultant firm in San Diego over ten thousand dollars to digitize Lottie's voice which had been recorded from her tapped phone. The supercomputer then composed the message Jess had heard telling him to meet her at her grandmother's cottage. It had only taken a well-placed bribe to get Jess's unlisted satphone number. When Chen called the boy, he had used a cutout that mimicked Lottie's number on the satphone's caller ID. The detective was banking on the fact that Jess had the phone's ringer turned off and that he wouldn't answer. If he had, Lottie's number would have appeared on the satphone's tiny screen, and the whole plan would have gone down the drain because there would be no one to talk to the boy. Fortunately, for Chen, Jess didn't answer—as usual. With the aid of his own caller ID to identify Jess's return call, Chen had switched the cutout on immediately, and the bogus message was played intead of Lottie's usual answering machine message. Lottie never knew what was going on.

When Chen had first found out from the news media that Jess was in the area, he had sent Halfsnake to replace the four-man team that had been watching the cottage. The Indian had watched with amusement when Nathan's surveillance crew had shown up, too. Discouraged, Nathan had pulled them after only seven days.

Several days later the Indian had spotted Jess when the boy had first arrived and made camp across the lake. Had they been able to depend on the young giant showing up on his own, all the electronic wizardry would have been needless. Chen was hedging his bets by using the fake message to get Jess within range of Halfsnake's transponder trick. The device would allow Chen to track the boy no matter where he went. When Jess was tracked for two days on the same state trail, Chen flew Ursala in by helicopter and dropped her where it would be impossible for the young giant to miss her. Her job was going to be the hardest—talk the boy into using his talent to heal a "friend." With Ursala's abilities, Chen knew she wouldn't fail.

The young giant and the tall woman talked about everything. Ursala had, indeed, spent several years modeling. She told him that she now worked as a troubleshooter for a blue-chip company on Wall Street. Jess couldn't pin her down any further on her job. They talked about schools, sports, music, and a hundred other things. It seemed that many of Jess's interests were shared by the dark-haired woman. She was extremely intelligent and well educated. It was on the fourth day that she broke both legs.

Totally unimpressed with Jess's unusual intelligence and accomplishments, she seemed to enjoy putting him down, especially if it involved flirting with danger. If there was a dangerous way to do something and a safe way to do it, she'd inevitably choose the dangerous, walking across a deep ravine on a rotten tree, body surfing the white water rapids of a river, swinging on a vine from a tree off a cliff to let go forty feet above the lake.

The result was to draw Jess closer and closer to her, and the closer he got, the more he wanted to impress her. She was sexy, provocative, although not a deliberate tease, and altogether an extremely sensuous looking and acting woman. She never mentioned sex. They slept in separate sleeping bags, and Jess did not see her naked again. However, he began to long to see her that way. The guard he'd kept in place all his life was beginning to fray a little. And Lottie was fading into the distance.

They had been climbing an eighty-foot limestone cliff to avoid walking around a large swamp. Ursala had suggested that they hike due east to Saratoga where she knew a horse trainer who would be racing a horse in two weeks. They could easily make the trek in that amount of time, but now there was a deadline, and the extra distance represented time.

Jess had balked at the climb, but Ursala had cajoled him into it.

"Pansy."

"I ain't no mountain climber."

"Why don't you walk around then? I'll wait for you when I get to the top—probably take a nap—or two."

"Do you always get your way?"

"Only when I want to."

Thirty feet up the cliff, she'd lost her hold and without so much as a whimper, she'd silently plunged to the rocks at the bottom. When Jess reached her, she was barely conscious and lay looking at him as if she had just won the national award for dumbness.

She must have landed on her feet. Both calves were bent at strange angles. When Jess reached beneath her right calf, his hand came away with blood on it. Looking closer he found the compound fracture. Broken ends of both the tibia and the fibula had come through the skin. There was also blood on the back of her head. She could easily have a concussion. Out of disgust at not getting a call from Lottie, he'd left the satphone with the bike. There'd be no helicopter to pick them up.

Her face was badly distorted as she said through gritted teeth, "Well, Kid, you'd better shoot me and put me out of my misery. I have no intention of letting you carry me." It was the last thing she said before she passed out.

As with the shepherd, in Germany, Jess panicked. What else could he do but take a chance on her discretion? It wasn't like he could heal her and leave before she woke up. He could pack her out on a litter, but there was extremely rough terrain in every direction and the nearest road was over twenty miles away. Without painkillers or antibiotics it was within the realm of possibility that she could actually die.

Because he had been so strongly drawn to her physically, Jess's reasoning was clouded. There was one last internal wave of compulsion that told him not to reveal his ability to this woman. In fact, each day there had been a little scratching at the back of his mind that told him being with her at all was wrong. It had never occurred to him to read her mind. Briefly the thought came and went that he could put her on a slow-heal, suppress the pain, and then camp for a few days until he could drag her out on a litter. But that wasn't what he wanted to do. He wanted to break through that aloofness; he wanted to make a dent in that invulnerability. Here was a chance to show her what he could do; here was a chance to outgun the enemy.

He reached down to the mangled legs, one at a time, and said softly, "Let the healing begin." It only took him a minute to straighten and repair both legs. He searched the wound at the back of her head, and finding several hairline fractures in her skull, he easily mended them along with the cut in her scalp.

Finally, he treated her brain so it would not swell from the trauma. When he'd finished, there wasn't the slightest hint of a wound.

She woke up a few minutes later and he was sitting a few feet away looking at her.

"Is this downtown Cleveland?"

He said nothing. There was a strong feeling that what he had just done was wrong. He'd never experienced feeling guilty over helping someone before.

Ursala sat up and reached for her legs.

"Wait a minute! Something isn't right here."

Jess was still silent.

"I know I had two broken legs. I heard them snap. Before I passed out, I saw the crazy angles."

Silence.

"What'd you do to me while I was out? Exactly what happened here?"

It was the most emotion he'd seen her show.

"Beats me. You up for a little roller skating?"

She stood up.

"They said . . ." She was unable to shake the shock from her face.

"What?"

"I didn't be—. . ."

"You're mumbling, woman. Delirious?"

"Jess! I know I had two broken legs a few minutes ago! Now I don't! And I certainly don't see Jesus Christ and His band of angels lingering in the trees. Now, what happened?" More animation.

"Maybe He was a little closer than you thought, Ursala." He sighed, stood up and said, "I have a special gift. That's why Uncle Sam was after me. They use me to heal the president and all his friends. I got bored and left."

"You did this for me knowing I could . . . You big fool, you don't even know me. You don't know what . . ." She was shaking her head, her voice tender. She gently reached for his face with one hand and studied his eyes. Then she stood on her tiptoes pulled him down to her and kissed him lightly on the mouth. "Thanks, Jessie." For one brief moment, the tough facade had been dropped. Then, like a closing drape, the hardness returned. She released him and said, "Let's go watch a horse race."

# 13

The next couple of days Jess became more and more desirous of Ursala. He knew he wasn't in love with her, and he knew those kind of feelings were wrong for him. They were feelings he'd always been able to handle, put out of his mind. She began to touch him more and more. She would stroke his chest, the small of his back. Sometimes even his rear end. He liked it. Sometimes she'd place his hand on her—the curve of her hip, her knee, her neck.

On the third night Jess felt if he didn't leave her and go his own way he was going to get into trouble. But leaving was not what he wanted to do, and he pushed it from his mind. The next day as she preceded him up a long mountain trail, he couldn't keep his eyes off her.

That night they lay a foot apart, silent, listening to each other's breathing. The darkness filled with the lonely invitations of crickets, frogs, owls, and other animals as they awakened and either proclaimed jubilations for still being alive or curses for a sun not yet risen. Jess wanted badly to kiss her but didn't dare. Finally she rolled over and kissed him, the full length of her body leaning against his, her near leg gripping him across his thighs. Jess was shocked at his own eagerness and the strength with which he grabbed her. The kissing grew harder quickly, and movements became more and more violent as competing passions strained to outdo each other. By the time the young giant realized what was happening, the dam had broken, and the waters it had held so long, so well, were lost forever.

The next morning, Jess felt the most wretched he'd ever felt in his life. The guilt overwhelmed him in waves. But the waves weren't high enough to stop him from making love to Ursala again. Or again that afternoon. Or again that night . . . Or again . . . Or . . .

Over the next few days the special times he spent communing in his seasons stopped. He was completely consumed by the newfound passion. Had someone told him a few days before—in his storeroom hideout when he was spending hours each day in communion, drawing power directly from the source for the amazing gifts that had been entrusted to him—had they told him he would throw that closeness away for this, he'd have told them they were crazy.

While they were hiking that afternoon, Ursala began to gently quiz him about his miracle power. When he told her of some of the miracles that he'd performed she became silent. In fact, she said nothing for several hours.

Finally, he could stand it no longer and said, "Ursala, did I say something that disturbed you? Why so quiet?"

"It's nothing."

There was another hour of silence and again Jess asked, "Something's wrong. You can't go this long without at least saying 'Ouch,' from the three times I've seen you stub your toe."

"Forget it."

"No. Out with it. I need to know what's bugging you."

They had been walking through a beautiful stretch of hardwoods. The trail was well-worn. They were only a mile or so from Whitehouse, where it ended. She stopped, turned around, and said, "Let's sit down."

There was a large dead tree next to the trail. They sat beside each other and she began, "I never knew who my father was. He left my mom when I was born. There was an older man living next door to us who had never been married. He took a liking to me and over the years he became the father I'd never had. I grew to love him just as if he were my own dad. My mother was a waitress. There was no way she could put me through college. Charles took it upon himself to do it for her, and after several years of sacrificing to pay my tuition, he was there when I graduated from Vassar."

She became silent again.

"And . . ."

"And, one of the reasons I came up here was to deal with the fact, in my own way, that he's dying of terminal cancer. It's inoperable. He's got weeks, at best."

"Where is he?"

"They sent him home from the hospital to die. He moved not long after I graduated. He lives in Kingston, down the Hudson. It's sixty, seventy miles from here."

"Why don't we rent a car and go see him?"

"What? Why?"

"Let me see if I can't fix him. It would not be the first time, and so far I've got a perfect record."

"Jess, you mean . . . You can heal him? You'd do this? For me?"

"Why not? It's what I do."

Chen had determined that it would be best to move the crusty old millionaire to a lower middle-class neighborhood not too far from where Ursala was doing her act. It would allay all kinds of suspicions and make the story and performance that Ursala was giving completely credible. However, it had not been easy containing the old man's gripes.

"Where is she? She's had a week. I'm not getting any stronger. For what we're paying her, she should have had him here days ago."

"Mr. Calhoun, this is a very delicate operation. If this boy suspects for a second that he's being set up, he won't heal you; and he is a very bright fellow. We also know that he would not do it for money no matter how much you offered him."

"Well, you'd better get in touch with her and tell her she'd better get a move on it. I'm going to be dead by the time she stops fooling around!"

"Her transponder says they have just come out of the mountains, sir. I expect to hear from her shortly. You just do your acting job when she gets here. Your life depends on it."

Two hours later the phone rang.

"Chen."

"We're on the way. It's worked like you wouldn't believe. We're at a rest stop on the thruway—about an hour away."

"We're ready. Let's keep our fingers crossed nothing goes wrong."

Over two dozen people had been involved in getting Ursala and Jess together and then monitoring them in the woods. They included the backpacker Jess had passed on the first part of the trail before he met Ursala, along with trackers and spotters all through the woods. There was even a helicopter on standby in case of some emergency. Chen almost pulled the plug when Ursala broke her legs. She was supposed to come up with an injury, but two broken legs and a serious concussion was overdoing it a bit. Fortunately, he didn't have to call the helicopter.

An hour later, in a suburb of Kingston, the couple pulled into the driveway of a nondescript ranch-type home that needed paint. Chen met them at the door in the guise of a male nurse who stayed with the old man on a part-time basis. Jess was led into the bedroom where Calhoun lay in a full-size bed with a beat-up wooden headboard.

"Ursala, Honey!"

The old man appeared too weak to sit up, and Ursala went to him and hugged him.

Since there was no reason to intrude on the privacy of Ursala's benefactor, Jess never read the old man's mind. He remained completely unaware of the monstrous deception, and he put the millionaire on a slow-heal. Calhoun would be feeling like a teenager inside three weeks. When they got back in the car, and he'd told Ursala that her friend was healed of every disease he had, she grabbed him and began kissing him so intensely, Jess had to pull the car to the side of the road.

"Let's find a motel. I can't take this!"

"Can you crawl into the back seat, Sport?"

They spent the night in a Holiday Inn. Ursala gave him her divided attention. She couldn't keep her mind off the fact that once Calhoun was healthy she would be, not one, but two million dollars richer.

She had brought it off, and it had been a piece of cake! The boy had never known what hit him.

The next day they drove to Lake George where Jess lucked out and was able to rent a cottage on the lake. They would spend the few days before the horse race relaxing. Chen had instructed Ursala to maintain the relationship until the old man had completely recovered in case something went wrong. When he was completely healed, she'd get paid.

Jess was having the time of his life and the guilt trips were becoming less intense. He'd had to wire the bank in Switzerland for more money. The cottage, complete with thirty-foot sailboat, was a thousand dollars a day, but what was that to a millionaire. Other than his boat, he'd never spent any serious money on just having fun. It was about time he started. Besides, Ursala was the kind of woman who would expect only first-class treatment. Hadn't she done modeling layouts all over the world? The only problem was that Jess had to be very careful about being seen. Uncle Sam had eyes all over the place.

They watched the race from the infield with Ursala's friend. Jess had dug out a custom-made full beard and thick moustache he kept tucked away in his pack. Immediately after the races were finished, they headed the rental car for I-87 and drove straight through to New York and Ursala's apartment. They remained in New York only long enough for Ursala to pack and for Jess to buy a few clothes and the disguise items necessary to make him look like one of his fake passport photos.

Then they flew to Paris.

"Paris is most romantic in the summer, not the spring."

They took the Orient Express to Istanbul, sleeping in an elaborate stateroom.

They spent a week in Rome.

Then Tangiers.

Including clothes and jewelry, Jess went through almost half a million dollars in a little over a month. The disguise was a nuisance he decided to do without. Instead of using the airlines he began chartering planes—usually a Lear. Meals were eaten in hotel rooms or in darkened corners of expensive restaurants. The boy didn't think Nathan would be looking for him in the kinds of places they frequented to shop.

They finally flew home the beginning of September. It had been almost a year since he'd seen Lottie. When he wired the Swiss bank for more money, he was horrified to find out that his account had been frozen. Uncle Sam had put a lien on it. Somehow Nathan had managed to trace the account number, and in recent years the Swiss government had become much more cooperative with the U.S. because of so many drug dealers.

Jess used his satphone to call the head of the National Security Agency.

"Nathan, this is not right. This is theft, unadulterated grand larceny! I earned that money!"

"Hey, Jessie! It's good to hear you. How's the mountain vacation going? Where are you by the way?"

"Nathan, I want that account unfrozen or I'll go to the press and tell them exactly what we've been doing. When they find out your boss has been getting his cold cures from a kid miracle-healer, the country will laugh him out of office; they won't even have to impeach him."

"Jess, I'm sorry you're so upset. Come back to work and we'll release the accounts. I already told you that we'll only call on you occasionally. You can stay at home."

"And I've told you before that I don't trust you. Your boss decides to get even with me and put me back on ice, you'll do it and say, 'Anything else, kind sir, Mr. President?' I'll die of starvation before I'll ever go through that again. Now release the funds or I talk to the *Post*."

"I don't think so, Jessie. If you were to do that, I'd have to release a lot of pictures and personal information. We could string the story out for years. There wouldn't be a place on God's green Earth where your face wouldn't be ten times more familiar than Elvis's."

"You wouldn't dare."

"What would I have to lose, Jessie?"

Jess knew the little man from Brooklyn would do exactly as he said he would.

In the next month and a half, Jess cleaned out the accounts in the small banks around the country where he'd stashed emergency money. He continued to entertain Ursala, sparing nothing. They went to Broadway plays, him in light disguise, her wearing the jewelry and expensive clothes he kept forcing on her. He knew it was foolish, but like an old man with a young woman, he just couldn't stop buying her gifts. She paid him back in bed each night.

Emptying the last account in a small bank in Nebraska sneaked up on him. He had refused to believe he could run out of money—it had always come so easy. However, the gravity of the situation began to sink in—he really was cut off. How was he going to support Ursala in the manner to which she had become accustomed?

It was Ursala who finally came up with an answer to the stewing and fuming that had gone on for days. They had been staying in her Manhattan apartment. She was having too much fun to leave him quite yet. Besides, Chen had only given her half her payment. "Wait another couple of weeks, Ursala. Let's make sure he's not going to have a relapse." She was angry, but there was nothing she could do about it. She knew the detective was good for the money. Also, there was the interesting proposition Chen had made the last time she'd talked to him on the phone. If she could pull it off, she could make a bloody fortune!

"Jess, do you remember the man who was the nurse for Charles?"

"Yeah. He was Oriental. Seemed like a nice enough guy."

"Well, my family has known him for a long time. He's Charles's friend—that's why he was taking care of him—but, ordinarily, he works only for a few very wealthy people—the ones who live in the hundred-acre estates along the Hudson—old New York money. What could be wrong with asking him if he knew someone who would pay for your services?"

"Ursala, I've never used my power for money! That would be perverted, hideously wrong!" He was getting red in the face, on the verge of shouting.

"Now wait a minute. You let Uncle Sam study you for $x$ amount of dollars. What's the difference?"

"That was different. They were trying to find out how to duplicate the ability."

"Baloney. You got paid to heal the president and all those other diplomats. It's exactly the same."

"No. It wasn't and I don't want to talk about it. I won't do it; it's a closed subject." But Jess wasn't sure if it really was a closed subject. She was right. He had been paid for his powers. Now they had stolen his earnings. There really was no way he could go back to work for Nathan. After making a fool out of the president of the United States, no telling what they'd do to him. Even if he could find a job at age nineteen—one that was compatible with his knowledge, Uncle Sam would be on him like mud on an August hog. He wasn't about to sponge his money off Ursala, and he certainly couldn't go home and live with Mom and Dad.

"Jess, doctors get paid." Ursala ignored the coming tantrum.

"Doctors had to earn their healing rights. Mine were given to me."

"By whom?"

"That doesn't matter right now."

"Let me call Chen and see what he could come up with. I don't in any shape or manner see anything wrong with taking payment from somebody who has so much money they literally don't know what to do with it. They may be dying; they can't take it with them. There are thousands of people who would give millions in return for their lives. You'd be providing them with happiness and health as opposed to misery and death."

"It's not right. Maybe they're supposed to die." But she could see he was weakening and Jess knew it. A couple of months before he would have had no doubts about selling his abilities. But life was no longer black and white. He was now finding that most of it was gray.

They had been sitting on the living room sofa. She stood, went to the table next to the phone, and pulled her address book out of her purse.

"I'm going to call and ask. You've nothing to lose."

Chen answered on the first ring. They talked. He already had the first patient in mind if Ursala could talk the young giant into it. A wall street financial baron was dying of lung cancer. The man was only in his sixties and according to Forbes he was worth in excess of five hundred million dollars. Chen would talk to the man's lawyer and set up the deal. No cure, no pay. They couldn't turn that down. A cure ought to be worth at least a tenth of what the man was worth.

Half an hour later, he called Ursala back and asked to talk to Jess. Jess was reluctant, but it wouldn't hurt to listen.

"Jess, I understand the way you feel." The detective's voice was soothing, not condescending, and what he said next was very persuasive. "J. John Burtland is worth in excess of half a billion dollars. If you just ease his pain he will pay you one million dollars. If you wait more than a few days, he very well may be dead! He's that close to dying. If you don't want the money, then give it to charity."

Jess thought to himself, *And where does it all go from here? We open Pandora's box, that's for sure.* However, he was broke. After the fifty dollars in his billfold was gone, he would have to call home to get his folks to send him money. Fifty dollars in the Big Apple might pay for parking for one day.

"Let me think about it."

The logic was overwhelming. Uncle Sam had paid him to heal. Jess hadn't asked for this gift. He had been born with it. In many ways it had been a curse. He'd been denied a normal life; he'd had to practice deception even in high school; he'd had to sneak around like some kind of criminal. What would be wrong with getting paid for easing pain and saving lives? In order to remain free it took a great deal of money. He wasn't like normal people who could walk the streets.

He thought about it a total of five hours. "Okay, Ursala, you win. Call Chen. Tell him I'll do it. Ask how much the old man will pay for a full-blown premium heal. In for a penny, in for a pound."

When it comes to life and death, the rich and famous don't waste any time. Jess was at the man's bedside that evening. Chen was paid partly in cash—straight from the back of a Brinks truck—and partly with an assortment of bearer bonds. He paid Jess two million dollars out of the cash. It was an enormous amount of money for two minutes of work. It was also a pittance for the multimillionaire, considering what he was getting in return. It would have taken Jess several months to make that much money healing the president and favored diplomats for Uncle Sam under the guise of a superficial study program designed to duplicate his skills. Ursala was paid one million. Chen was not entirely greedy, and he recognized how imperative it was to keep Jess on a string. The young giant now had enough money to resume his fling with his new girlfriend. However, the temptation to make more was overpowering. Pile it up; get enough to never have to prostitute his gift again—enough where "Uncle" couldn't interfere; then retire and enjoy it. It had been so unbelievably easy! Ursala made sure he didn't forget that—not for a single minute.

Two days later, Chen had another patient. This one would be worth even more. Jess quickly said yes. Perhaps he would use some of the money to help others who were in need.

The deal was made to heal another cancer-ridden multimillionaire, and payment would be in cash. Because the millionaire had no connections with the banking business, it took him two days to raise the funds. Jess walked away with another two million. Now he had a problem—how to launder the money without Uncle Sam finding him. He fully intended to pay income tax on it, but stuffing it in a bank account would almost guarantee getting it frozen the same way they had locked away his Swiss accounts.

Chen gave him the name of a Manhattan law firm that helped him form a string of corporations that ranged from New York to Miami, from Indonesia to the Bahamas, the Caymans and beyond. For a healthy percentage they buried and invested the money so that no one would ever find it or the name of its owner. Because Jess kept a healthy chunk of cash to live on, it would be some time before he would learn that Chen's fingers were all over the deal. When the boy would finally try to liquidate, he would find himself left with only a few thousand dollars.

Over the next few weeks Chen set up over two dozen healings, each one netting the young healer a minimum of one million dollars. However, there was one very disturbing development. Jess decided to read the mind of one of his "patients" just to see what kind of a person the man really was. The young giant discovered that his mindreading power wouldn't work. He tried it on several other people over the next few days, and there was no doubt about it—the ability was gone. His seasons had become a forgotten part of the past. No longer did his conscience bother him about sleeping with Ursala or taking money for his services. Why should it? After all, he wasn't sleeping around, and wasn't he doing the exact same thing with his miracle ability that he had done for Uncle Sam?

Chen continued to line up wealthy clients. There was no end to them. Twice they flew to Europe on private jets to heal billionaires—one in London and one in Greece. However, each time he used the power, Jess found it became a little harder to make it work.

They were in Ursala's apartment in Manhattan discussing the patient scheduled for the following afternoon. They had just flown in the night before from Las Vegas where Jess had healed a famous entertainer of AIDS and had restored the man's hair.

Jess said, "Chen, I need a break. It's getting harder and harder for me to bring these things off. For some reason, my power is diminishing. Maybe some rest will bring it back."

Chen and Ursala looked at him like he had the plague. Here was the golden goose coming down with constipation.

Chen finally said, "Jess, some of these people may die at any time. It's hard to see them in such desperate need, know that we can save their lives, and not extend our help. However, if you feel it's absolutely necessary, let's do the one we have scheduled for tomorrow, then you can take a couple days off."

The next afternoon the three of them were in the mansion of a sixty-four-year-old lady who had been the heiress to a cosmetics fortune. She was worth hundreds of millions of dollars. She was willing to pay ten million dollars to have Jess remove facial wrinkles and varicose veins. She was a hyper-allergic to every anesthesia known to man—both general and topical. For her to tolerate any kind of surgery was a major undertaing and extremely dangerous.

By now, the pretext of a slow heal was useless. Besides, it complicated getting paid. By word of mouth alone, news of the boy's miraculous talent was spreading like wildfire. The cliques of the rich knew that the six-foot-ten-inch giant was performing life-saving miracles, and they did not want to wait to get better. Neither did Chen want to wait for his money. And like so many other things, the rich and famous were more than adept at keeping this incredible windfall for themselves. The media would never get the slightest whiff of what was going on. Why share this priceless gift with the commoners? It might mean waiting in line the next time.

They were seated in green leather chairs in the mansion's library. Jess was speaking. "Mrs. Meyer, do you have any other internal problems that you know about?"

She hesitated. It wasn't easy for most people to expose themselves.

"Kidney stones. Most pain I ever went through in my life. Worse than all three kids stacked on top of each other at childbirth. Can you fix that too?"

"I'm sure I can." Ordinarily, Jess would have been able to tell everything that was wrong with the woman by just shaking her hand. He had been able to tell nothing. Chen was about to interrupt to demand more money, but Jess's look stopped him. The young giant got to his feet and approached the woman.

"Just let me put my hand on your forehead and see if we can't put everything in order."

He held his hand in place for the better part of a minute. Then he shifted it to the top of her head. Then the back of her neck. For five minutes he placed his hands on her and the whole time the look of consternation on his face built. It turned to a controlled panic and he finally choked out, "It's gone!

I can't feel a thing. The power's gone! I'm sorry."
He backed away from her in slow horror.

Chen leaped to his feet with fire in his eyes. The
woman began to cry softly.

"I'm sorry. I am so sorry. I'm sorry . . ." Jess was
still babbling as they led him out of the room.

As they got into the car to leave, he barely heard
Chen say, "Mrs. Meyer, he's been under a tremendous amount of strain. We'll give him a few days off.
As soon as his power returns I promise you'll be the
first one he sees."

Chen was wrong. The power did not return—not
after a few days—not after a few weeks! The young
giant sulked around Ursala's apartment when he
wasn't in bed. He said nothing. They were unable to
get him to go out; they were unable to get him to
eat. The horror in his mind was beyond belief. For
the first time in his life he was no longer special. He
was alone, helpless, gutted. He was not very interested in living.

Two months went by and there was no doubt in
Jess's mind—he was permanently useless. He had
prostituted himself and the payback was as inevitable as day and night.

It was early January. The entire week had been
overcast. At exactly four o'clock the sun appeared
briefly and bounced carelessly off thousands of
Manhattan windows. Pewter light soaked the furniture nearest the apartment windows, leaving the

remainder of the room to the devices of soft indirect lighting. Jess was sitting on the sofa staring at the TV with the volume turned off.

Ursala put on her coat and said, "I've got to do some grocery shopping. I'll be back in about an hour." She left the door cracked and did not even bother to look at him. There never had been any feeling for Jess—or anyone else, for that matter. Ursala used people to arrange a more convenient life for herself. Rarely did emotion intrude on her life. She had not been traumatized as a child; there'd been no molestation, no beatings or mental abuse. She'd grown up in a middle-class neighborhood in Albany. As long as she could remember—grade school, high school, college, work—there had been little in the way of emotions.

When she was twelve, she had been helping her mother slide a large trunk down the attic stairs. It slipped. She managed to step aside, but the trunk and her mother bounded down the entire length of the stairs. In the space of one minute, she'd silently watched her mother fade and die of a crushed rib cage. There had been little more emotion than if the woman had dropped a plate while washing the dishes. It wasn't something Ursala solicited; she'd simply been born with a meager dose of emotion-driving hormones.

Money had eventually become the most important thing in her life. This boy had been an investment while he'd lasted. Jess had never heard the arguments she'd had with Chen to increase her share. "Why don't you baby-sit him then, Chen? See if you can find him when you want him? Either ante up or I'm leaving." Chen had. She was now a very wealthy woman.

The familiar rusty voice came to Jess from the apartment's doorway: "Jess, how you doin'? So nice to see you again. Great place you got here. Nice view. I used to live over that way a couple miles."

Jess turned to find Nathan standing there, infectious smile and all. There were two large men on either side of him. One of them was holding a set of handcuffs. Chen had bargained the little Brooklyn agent up to a hundred thousand dollars. Ursala would get half.

# 14

Under decree of the president of the United States, who never gave up a grudge, Nathan had Jess returned to the safehouse and his old suite. At least now they could reason with the boy. Jess had folded even deeper within himself and didn't bother to tell the NSA head that the government's miracle worker was now out of business. Nathan did notify Jess's parents this time. They were relieved to hear about their errant son. Jess hadn't called them in weeks. What they were not happy about was Nathan not allowing them to see him.

"He's under observation. We're running some tests."

Jeff protested loudly, but both he and Stephanie knew that Uncle Sam could stonewall until the cows came home when he wanted to.

Three days later, Jess heard the helicopter. One of the guards came for him, and he was escorted downstairs where Nathan was waiting for him in the living room. The young giant had remained curled in a fetal ball on the bed the entire three days since he'd been brought back. He had eaten nothing. His weight was down sixty pounds from the last time he'd been in the house.

"Well, Jessie, you want to tell me about your adventures?"

No answer.

"We can keep you here as long as we like, you know."

Still no answer.

"I have a patient for you to heal if you'd like to move back into the congeniality suite. Helping somebody might do you some good, get you back on your feet. It looks like you haven't done so well over the past few months."

"Nathan, I've lost the power. I can't heal any more."

"Sure, and Lenin's grave is a Communist plot."

"Suit yourself."

Concerned over the boy's health, Nathan had Jess taken back to Walter Reed where Dr. Fielder was waiting with a few of the old staff.

"Jess, it's good to see you. Nathan told me you didn't look so hot, but I'll admit I wasn't prepared for this. How much weight have you lost?"

Jess said nothing.

"Okay. One of these days. Well, with or without your permission I'm going to run a few tests. You said you've lost your power?"

"Yes."

"Do you have any idea why?"

Jess returned to his silence. He refused to answer all but the most basic questions the entire week he remained in the hospital. He allowed them to poke and prod. He couldn't care less. Nathan called Fielder every day to find out if his prize hound was going to be able to hunt. At the end of five days, the doctor told him that there were, indeed, some drastic changes in the boy's body in comparison to its former state.

"He may be telling the truth, Nathan. He may have lost his abilities."

"Could he be faking it?"

"You can't fake an EEG. You can't fake your body chemistry. His metabolism and blood are nothing like they were a year ago, and we certainly spent enough time establishing benchmarks. I think he's telling the truth."

"Do you think he'll talk to me?"

"If he won't talk to me, he won't talk to you. I suggest you kick him loose. Send him home. Maybe it'll turn things around. I have no idea what he's been through, or why he's lost his power. Maybe his folks can pry it out of him."

"What a waste. I suppose if he gets it back we could always collect him again."

"I'm sure you could try."

The next day Dr. Fielder called Stephanie. She was shocked to find out that Jess had been in the same hospital where she worked, and she was apprehensive when Fielder told her she could take him home. She bombarded the doctor with questions, but all he could tell her was that there were a lot of changes that had taken place in Jess's body, that the boy said he no longer could heal, and that Uncle Sam was letting him go. No more wanted posters behind post office counters.

Once he was home and in his own room, Jeff and Stephanie left him alone. The young giant spent a lot of time in bed but did begin to eat. No one could resist Rainbow Trout ala Stephanie for very long. After three weeks of doing nothing and answering only a few questions, Jess finally appeared one morning for breakfast—unusual.

"Where's Dad?"

"He left early to drive to Hampton. He's working on the licensing applications for a new mall. How are you feeling?"

"Better, but I need some time alone, Mom. I think I'll go back to the mountains."

"The Adirondacks?"

"Yeah."

"Jess, it's in the dead of winter! It goes down to forty below up there. You'll freeze!" Stephanie was spooning scrambled eggs on his plate to go with the four patties of sausage that were waiting. He had made himself four pieces of toast and spread half a jar of strawberry jam on them. At least he was eating again.

"Naw. The Cherokee's still in a garage in Ottawa.

I'll fly up, buy the winter equipment I need, and then do some hiking. It'll be pretty. There hasn't been a lot of snow."

"You'll take the phone?"

"Yes."

"And call me every day?"

"Certainly."

"Why can't you hike around our own mountains here in Virginia?"

"I like the Adirondacks. It's pure wilderness up there. Here I keep running into farms and villages."

Stephanie knew it would be useless to argue. Jess was not normal—not like other kids, and the boy had always seemed to know best how to get out of his own predicaments. However, he'd never tackled anything like this one before. At least he wouldn't have to sneak home any more.

Two days later, he left the Jeep at a gas station in the tiny sprinkling of homes called Santa Clara and turned his back on civilization. That night he put up the winter tent and made camp next to an inlet on the shore of a frozen pond. The area had just completed its mandatory January thaw. Most of the snow had melted from the woods, and ponds and lakes, now ironed smooth, were awaiting fresh frosting. The full moon quietly scattered pale-crystal sparks across the ice as if a chandelier had exploded and lay strewn. Temperature was in the high twenties.

Once more the young giant went to work trying to regain the favor of his seasons, his source, but the communion still eluded him. He spent hours reading by the light of a battery-operated lantern and trying harder and harder to communicate. The deep-freezer quiet of the mountains was broken only by a hunting wildcat and a few sleepless chickadees.

"Please! I am sorry. I have royally failed! This separation is slowly and surely eviscerating me." It was the thousandth time he'd asked for help.

Nothing.

The lack of condemnation was there; that was a given. It had been paid for with an astronomical price, but there was no communion.

Toward dawn, there was a touch of contact. A small probe. It gave him the strength to continue. He stayed in the tent the whole day, asking, searching, reading the familiar verses, claiming the old promises. About midnight there was another touch. It gave him the impetus to continue through the night again. He had gone without food for two days.

"I will not disappoint you again. Please return your presence so I can be of use. I don't deserve my gifts back."

Nothing.

He drifted off to sleep and upon awaking, found the propane heater had run out of fuel. He replaced the tank with a fresh one and was surprised to see that his watch said it was almost noon. He'd slept half of the day away. When he stepped outside the tent, he was pleasantly surprised. There had been a light dusting of snow. The clouds had come, worked quickly, and left again. The sky was mostly clear except for some high altocumulus scud. A woodpecker was hard at work across the pond. Its irregular volleys echoed through the woods like the rhythms of a bad but determined typist. Jess decided to go for a walk. The snow had sterilized the scene, blotting out nature's blights and imperfections.

He'd walked the better part of three miles, deeply involved once again in finding the familiar arms, warmth, breath. As he crested a small hill, he was startled back to reality by red spots on the snow.

"Blood."

He followed the trail into a thick stand of white birch, and there, lying on its side, was a small buck. It opened its eyes as he approached, but it was much too weak to protest. The pain in the umber eyes cut the boy to the bone. There was a large blood smear down the side of the animal's beautiful coat in the area of the stomach.

"Not even in season and gut shot! The guy didn't even have the decency to follow you and finish the job."

The deer stirred only a little when Jess reached out his hands and placed them tenderly on its fur. Carefully he probed for the pain. A few months ago the ability to restore the animal would have been as perfunctory as eating lunch. Watching it bound away would have been the highlight of the week.

Tears welled up in Jess's eyes, and the clinker in his throat burned hotter and hotter. This animal's pain was inexcusable. The boy cried out in anguish, "Please, let me fix him! He didn't do anything!"

Determined, Jess began to concentrate, to focus all his faculties in order to bring them to bear on the life-giving force that would quietly funnel from his hands into the poor animal's pain.

Nothing happened.

He concentrated harder. Drops of sweat began to crawl down his face in spite of the cold. He gritted his teeth, eyes scrunched tightly closed. An extended, low groan escaped, framing the effort as the young healer concentrated harder and harder. His ears rang with racing blood. He could not quite feel the animal's life force, but it was close, only just out of reach. He snarled and snapped his head in greater concentration. Blood sang louder and louder in his ears in fits and jolts.

"Pleassssssssse!"

He began breathing in great gulps to feed the rhythmic growls that came involuntarily with greater and greater concentration. He hardly felt the soft snaps through his body as more and more capillaries blew with the inhuman effort.

It culminated with one long, loud, spine-chilling scream.

"AAAAAAaaaaaaaaggggghhhhhhh!"

The circuit breakers finally blew, and the boy was thrown to the ground in great convulsions. Arms and legs jerked involuntarily and small rocks and twigs were displaced from winter's frozen aspic. The seizure mercifully ended in unconsciousness as the young giant gently folded across the deer. When he woke three hours later, the animal was cold and Jess could not feel his own fingers and toes. Ax-blow paroxysms split his head in pain that had yet to be classified among the living. Every muscle in his body was being hosed with large blowtorches, and his stomach felt like he'd swallowed a gunnysack of very active worms. Between the first and second bouts of vomiting, it took only a few seconds for the young giant to realize that it wasn't night and totally dark—he was totally blind!

"Oh, Father, no!"

For half an hour he could only rock in the muddy snow on his hands and knees, holding his fragmenting head with enough pressure to squeeze a horse to death. And silently scream!

Panic gradually sat in as the pain gradually seeped away.

As he felt the afternoon sun cool, renewed fears scampered around inside his head like fall chipmunks.

Then it got cold.

When the pain had finally diminished enough so that he could stand, Jess tried walking slowly by feeling ahead with his hands and feet. It took him half an hour to get out of the alder thicket. There were a few yards of open space, then he felt himself begin to climb.

"It must be right. I remember coming down a hill when I was tracking the deer."

Slipping and sliding to his knees over and over on snow-greased leaves, he climbed until he felt level ground.

"I've got to keep moving or I'll freeze." His clothes were soaking wet on the outside from the snow—on the inside from perspiration.

He was very cold. Thank goodness he'd put his gloves in his parka pockets when he'd taken them off to examine the deer. However, he'd long ago lost the little feeling that had returned to fingers and toes. The fact that he'd eaten nothing for two days didn't help.

He felt bare rock under his feet, and the trees disappeared. In the distance he could hear the trickle of a small stream. He was extremely thirsty and decided that following the stream might bring him to the lake. Slowly crabbing across the bare rock in a crouch, he was totally unprepared when his foot slipped on an angled slab. Before the young giant could fall to his hands and knees in defense, he was pitched onto his back to begin rapidly sliding down a very steep hill in utter helplessness. Jess groped desperately for a tree, a shrub—anything to stop the terror of not being able to see what was ahead. Terror changed to instant, heart-stopping panic when the ground suddenly disappeared beneath his feet, then kicking legs, then his back, then his head.

He shot off the cliff to spin into nothingness, and cold evening air snapped at him viciously for leaving terra firma.

For the second time, Jess awoke from unconsciousness with a loose jackhammer caroming around the inside of his head. Now it was *cold*—unbelievably cold! His teeth chattered uncontrollably as he groaned to his feet. The bizarre thought occurred to him that if he could get his mind started again—after this second trauma—he might hear its clicks and clinks echoing off the nearby trees and rocks. The sound of the stream slowly scrolled into his conscious, and with the water's crystal warbling came a wonderful shock—he could see!

"Thank you! I appreciate that."

There before him was the top of the cliff—over twenty-five feet high.

"Should have busted something. Can't believe I was that lucky." The tiny echoes of his voice swirled around the trees and bounced off the rock face.

His parka sleeve was badly ripped and soaking wet.

"Must have caught it in the stream."

No.

Although there was pain from one end of his body to the other, the most persistent stabbing came from the ripped-parka left arm. Probing brought a sharp yelp, and after taking his coat off, through giant blue sparks of pain, he could see through the rips in his sweater and shirt that there was a gaping ten-inch trough in his arm. Impossible to see red in the dark, the wetness that was supposed to be water was blood. Miraculously, it wasn't broken. The activity at least stopped his teeth from chattering.

"Lucky. Very lucky." It was a wonder with all the unconsciousness that he hadn't got frostbitten badly.

He folded his handkerchief and placed it the length of the wound. The cloth was quickly soaked. Pulling the drawstring from his hood, he tied the makeshift bandage in place. The parka went back on gingerly, and after pulling out the drawstring from around the hem, he wound it around his upper arm and half-cinched it with the help of his teeth. It would have to be loosened every few minutes.

"Ms. Lion and her illegitimate rabie—rabies." It was the same arm. How many centuries ago had that been?

The water from the brook was slightly bitter after steeping in fall's leaves for half the winter, but some of Jess's nausea and faintness had dissipated.

The moon slithered behind more and more clouds as it did its frame-by-frame dive for the horizon. An unidentifiable cry echoed somewhere in the distance, but night, or something else, abruptly choked it. The light on Jess's watch told him it was almost 3:30 A.M. He decided to follow the stream. It had to empty eventually into a pond or a lake. With a little luck it would be his pond. Slipping, falling, sometimes sliding off the bank to splash into shallow water, he followed the twists and turns through the woods. After walking for what seemed like an eternity, the gears of daylight began to creak and grate behind clouds that had gradually screened the full moon. It would snow before the day was barely birthed, and Adirondack snows could get serious. Jess tried to pick up his pace, but whenever he missed his step and his body was even slightly jolted, there were great flashes of bare-steel lightning that cavorted before his eyes. Not long after daylight he reached a pond, and it was his pond. It was not hard to locate the camp. With difficulty, he managed to get the propane heater lit, and within a few minutes the tent was toasty. He'd never been so thankful for anything in his life.

With the parka and shirts off, he got a good look at the wound. It was still bleeding and needed stitches. Obviously, an artery or vein had been severed. Weakened the way he was, Jess wasn't sure that he could walk out of the woods without resting first. But all the while he was resting, the gash would still be losing blood without a tourniquet. And leaving the string on for more than a few minutes invited old-fashioned gangrene. Jess rebandaged it with another handkerchief and put on a fresh shirt and sweater from his pack. When he removed the tourniquet, blood quickly and quietly appeared through the sleeve of the sweater.

Dealing with the cut would have been a little easier had he been carrying a first-aid kit. However, for his entire life, he had been the first-aid kit.

Reluctantly, he found his way to the brook that fed the cove where the moon had once danced. After half an hour's work and two frozen hands, he uncovered several hibernating crayfish under the stream's mud. Along with a smooth stone, he took them back to the tent, and after apologizing to the poor animals, he mashed their carapaces to a fine pulp in the bottom of a small pan. Along with some powder from a freeze-dried beef stroganof dinner and a little water, Jess made a paste to apply to the wound. Chemicals in the crayfishes' shells would form the basis for the hemostatic salve to stop the bleeding. Stitches could wait until he got to a doctor.

By three o'clock that afternoon he had downed three freeze-dried dinners and had been able to pack. Enough strength had returned that he was able to walk out of the woods and back to the Jeep in Santa Clara. There would be an emergency room at the hospital in Saranac Lake, which was about half an hour south. On the way, Jess checked the caller ID on the satphone. Someone had called from home a total of ten times. He called the familiar number and there was no answer. No answer at his dad's office either. By the time he was able to track down his mom at work, he'd just turned into the emergency room parking lot. Jess knew from the sound of his mother's voice that something was wrong. She reluctantly told her son that Lottie had been in a car accident. A drunk had hit her head-on, and she was not expected to live!

# 15

The bleeding finally stopped, and with assorted types of pain, faint and nauseated, Jess still made the trip from the far side of the Adirondack Mountains to Baltimore Memorial Hospital two hours under what would be normal. The Cherokee threatened to redline all the way, and, fortunately, there was not a cop in sight. By phone from the car, he tried all kinds of airline connections, but the bottom line was he could drive it as fast as he could fly. Also, there was always the chance of canceled or delayed flights.

It was almost 4 A.M. when he parked the Jeep in the parking lot and raced for one of the side entrances praying that it would be open. The exits for Albany had been flying by when he'd called his mother to find out Lottie's updated condition and her room number. The hospital had refused to give him any information by phone. Stephanie had called a friend at the hospital, then called Jess back. Obviously, Lottie's parents were at the hospital because repeated calls to their home went unanswered.

His mom's voice had come back sad and discouraged. "She's critical, Jess. Hurry! They don't expect her to make it through the night. And Jess?"

"Mom?" His voice was choked.

"I want you to hear this before one more minute goes by: That girl is one of the most precious creatures I've known on God's green earth. She was raped! That's how she got pregnant! She's got a set of morals and a love inside her that put yours to shame!" The tears he had held back so far now flowed freely. It had been all he could do to see the road at over one hundred miles per hour.

The side entrance was open! He had put on an old jacket to hide the blood on his sweater sleeve. Had anyone found him with a blood-soaked arm, they might have detoured him to the emergency room before kicking him out. By using the stairs, he made his way to the seventh floor. Peeking out the door, he saw only one nurse at the nurse's station, and when she mercifully turned her back to go to the files, Jess slipped silently around the corner. There was a sign that said, "Intensive Care Ward." The rooms down the hall had doorways but no doors. Each room was separated from the hall by a large window. The third doorway had a plaque on the casing that said 705. It was the room Jess was looking for, and he quickly disappeared inside.

Except for Lottie, the room was empty. Evidently, her folks were waiting in the visitor lounge. Jess was shocked at the number of tubes and wires that were hooked up to the young woman. Half a dozen monitors hiccuped and beeped at him without the slightest interest in his anguish. Apathetic green lines and grids exercised on black screens as they had for hundreds of other desperate loved ones who had watched and listened with nothing to do but hope, pray, and reflect.

She looked smaller than Jess had remembered. There was one chair in the room. As he sat down next to her in the semidark, he could see that her face was badly swollen and horribly discolored. He leaned forward and ever so gently kissed the face that had not allowed him a day's peace in over a year. He took his coat off and cupped her hand.

"Lottie, I love you." More soft-water tears.

The monitors answered him with diligent monotony.

Never in his entire life had Jess felt such debilitating helplessness. And never before had every cell in his body burned in such concentrated shame. His selfishness with Ursala, a woman for whom he cared little, or nothing, was probably going to cost Lottie her life.

But his power was gone. For weeks he had done his absolute best to get it back, and the effort had come within a millimeter of killing him. He still had a splitting headache from the attempt to heal the deer, and the untreated wound on his arm ached mercilessly. He would, without hesitation, try his power again if he thought there was even the slightest chance of restoring the girl. Unfortunately, they had made it arc-light clear. He had squandered the gift, had thrown it away on transient pleasure and an attempt at getting even instead of trusting. His punishment lay in the bed before him.

Jess had only been sitting for a few minutes when he was shocked out of his self-pity by the monotonous sound of the monitor shifting to a fluttered tone. He glanced at the screens, and a bolt of terror shot through him. The displays were all flat lines.

"Father, God, NO! Please no!"

The door to the room flew open, the lights came on, and two nurses ran to a stainless steel cart with a machine on it and dragged the cart across the floor. One of the women began hitting switches on the machine while the other pulled the sheet down to expose Lottie's bare upper chest. A doctor came running in and glanced at the EKG monitor. "She's in V-fib!" He opened Lottie's mouth briefly to make sure the airway was clear, breathed two breaths down her throat, mouth to mouth, then began CPR on her chest with his hands.

"Set it on two hundred. Get me one milligram of epinephrine and set up the sodium bicarb."

The nurse with the machine set a dial at two hundred joules and picked up the two paddles Jess had seen in the movies. The other nurse began preparing the solutions to inject into the IV. She turned to the young giant and said, "Who are you?

What are you doing in here this time of night?" Jess stood but didn't answer. He was still holding Lottie's hand.

"Kid, get out of my way or get out of the room!" Both doctor and nurses sensed that ordering the young giant to leave would be a waste of time. The doctor bumped him to one side, took the paddles from the nurse and placed them on Lottie's chest. Jess reluctantly let go and backed out of the way.

"Charged!"

"Hit it!"

The machine gave a short buzz that was followed immediately by a loud snap, and Lottie's body arched off the bed.

They all watched the monitors in concentrated hope.

Nothing.

"Set three hundred!" He handed the paddles back and resumed the CPR.

Thirty seconds later the nurse called, "Charged."

The doctor took the paddles back and cried, "Clear. Hit it!"

The process was repeated and once again they looked at the screens.

Nothing.

"Gimme a four hundred!" Again he resumed CPR as the crash cart recharged.

The shock was repeated again, but the monitors stubbornly remained flat.

"One milligram Lidocaine!"

They shocked the broken body five more times, each time after injecting a more potent drug into the IV. Hope melted from the trio like leftover Jell-O down a sink's drain. The doctor continued to pound on Lottie's chest hard enough to break bones, intermittently listening in short bursts with his stethoscope as if the monitors would lie.

After thirty minutes of concentrated effort he finally took the earpieces out, slowly folded the instrument, and put it in his coat pocket. He turned to the boy and said, "I'm sorry, kid—whoever you are. She was broken up worse than anyone I've ever seen. She really didn't have a chance. With the amount of electricity she's just endured, even if she'd made it back, she'd have severe brain damage. Judy, give him a few minutes. I'll go tell her folks."

Jess returned to the chair, sat, and once again took Lottie's hand. The trio left the room, one by one, leaving him with tears streaming down his face. The last nurse out barely heard him say, "Father . . ."

Once again he began to pray, to once more enter the season of communion with a Creator who had entrusted him with a gift, in measure, that had not been seen in nearly two thousand years. The gift had been taken back. So be it. He was far from worthy of using it anymore. All Jess wanted now was to feel the intimate presence and comfort of the One who had been so close for so long. Above all, sin separates, and Jess sorely missed that friendship. Within a couple of minutes the young giant was soaked in sweat from the concentration of trying to, once again, restore communications.

"Forgive me for costing her life. I know this may be a little unsound theologically, but please say hello for me. Please tell her how much I loved her.

"Savior, Precious Jesus, I know you forgive. Thank you. And thank you for all those people you did heal through me."

So tremendous was the young giant's concentration, he failed to notice a familiar feeling seeping into a body gone slack from the deepest grief. He certainly didn't feel it flow through him into the outstretched hand of the dead girl.

So intent was he on reaching his Creator, he didn't even hear the monitors that the nurse had forgotten to shut off. The green lines had lain still where they'd fallen as the monotones droned on helplessly. But now the lines began to ping and dance like the Phoenix from its ashes.

So deep was he in his search for a God he refused to believe had abandoned him, Jess failed to hear Lottie say, "Jess, you're hurting my hand."

She opened her eyes and saw him totally deflated—just an inert heap in the chair. The bedside was soaked from his tears. His head was down, but she knew his eyes were tightly shut. She knew where he was. She had made a practice of being there all her life just as he had. Funny they'd never talked about it. The difference was that she had not been given the same gifts or their responsibilities.

"Jess, I have never stopped loving you, and you are hurting my hand."

"Wh . . . ? Wh . . . ?"

The overpowering love with its incredible joy that he had been seeking for weeks softly exploded inside him an instant before he jerked his head up in utter shock. Lottie was smiling at him. With her other hand she reached, wiped the tears from his face, and said, "You heard me."

Both loves overwhelmed the young giant so totally he couldn't make the beginnings of speech. His surroundings swirled dizzily before him as if he'd just awakened from a five-year coma, and he had all he could do to keep from falling off his chair. With his mouth hanging open in disbelief, Jess's golden-brown eyes fiercely searched her face for the swelling and bruising that had been there moments before. However, the old Lottie smiled back at him. There wasn't a trace of an injury not only on her face but anywhere else on, or in, her body.

"Lottie!"

"Hey, Wonder Boy, welcome back."

"Lottie!"

"Would you get me the bathrobe hanging in the closet over there?"

"LOTTIEEEE!"

An hour and a half later the morgue still hadn't come for her body. Actually, no one yet knew that there no longer was a corpse. Jess had turned off the monitors. The couple stood in each other's arms at the window watching night's curtain slowly rise on one of dawn's most spectacular orange-pink fluorescent shows. Because of another crisis on the other end of the floor, Jess had been forgotten. Lottie had kept him from going to "fix" the patient. "Sometimes it's just time for them to go, Jess."

The gash on Jess's arm had disappeared along with every pain, including the headache. His miraculous gift had been returned. He was being given another chance.

"That's one of the hardest things to accept. Some people are not meant to be healed. I can't help them."

Lottie's parents had chosen to remember the girl as she was, rather than programming their memories with the way she looked, mangled, dead. Weeping, they had shuffled to their car and were on their way home. By the time they got there, the phone would be ringing, and they would be in for a shock.

The first ones to find out about the miracle were Jess's mom and dad. It had been an hour and a half's drive from where they lived. Stephanie was in her nurse's uniform—she was supposed to go on duty that morning. She had been in this hospital several times before, so she just led the way. As she and Jeff entered the room, she could see the outline of the couple against the window. There was no mistaking Jess's profile.

"Jeff, look!" She had spoken in a whisper.

She grabbed her husband, and tears began to flow from both of them.

"Jessie?"

"Mom?" The couple turned.

Stephanie ran for him and threw her arms around both him and Lottie.

"I knew! I knew!"

"You knew before I did, Mom."

"What happened to your arm? What's all this blood?"

She was fingering his sleeve.

"Well, there was a little scratch on it. It's gone."

"Lottie, look at you! I had a graphic medical description of your condition. There wasn't a prayer."

Lottie smiled at her and hugged the grinning young giant even tighter as she said, "Oh, there was a prayer. It had to complete a long, long journey around some serious stubbornness in order to get through, but there was always a prayer."

## ABOUT THE AUTHOR

Rick Gibson is a singer/songwriter who lives in the Nashville area. He is a graduate of Houghton College who has enjoyed writing for many years. *The Healer* is his first novel.